Joe Alex

THE SHIPS OF MINOS

Translated by
Adam Czasak

MONDRALA
PRESS

©1972-1975, 2002 The Estate of Maciej Słomczyński
©This English translation Adam Czasak, 2023
Originally published in Polish as *Czarne okręty* in 1972-75

Mondrala Press is an imprint of
Ringel & Esch, S.A.R.L.-S
www.mondrala.com

All rights reserved. No part of this book may be reproduced in any form whatsoever without permission in writing from the publisher, except for brief quotations in reviews.

ISBN Kindle: 978-2-919820-15-3
ISBN Paperback: 978-2-919820-16-0
ISBN Hardcover: 978-2-919820-17-7

Edited by Bill Allender
Cover Design by art_infinity

THE SHIPS OF MINOS

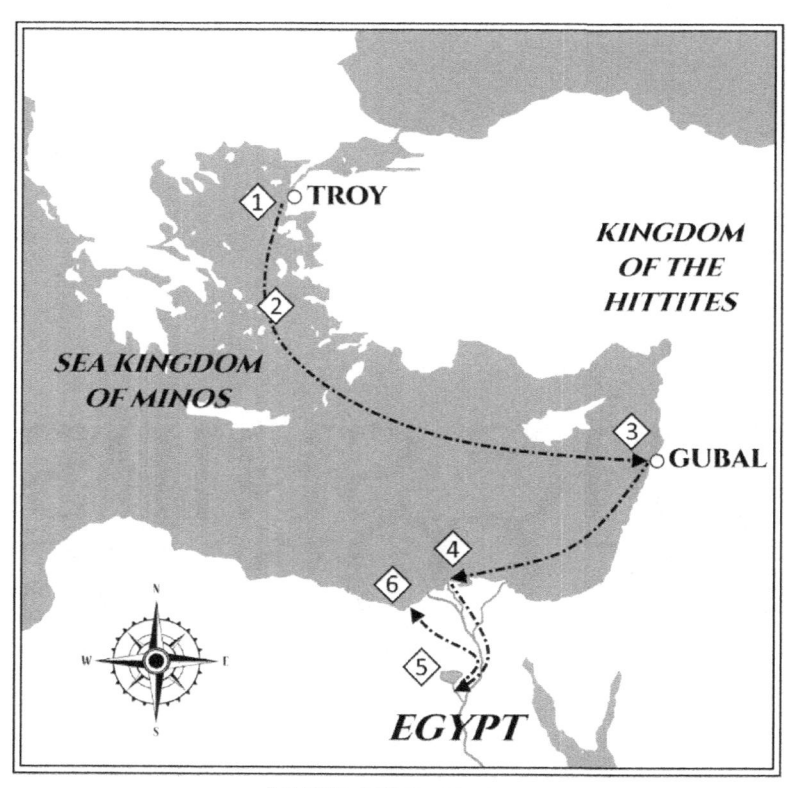

Volume 1
LET US OFFER HIS BLOOD UNTO OUR GODS

TABLE OF CONTENTS

CHAPTER ONE
Ida, Mountain of Our Forefathers, Be Kind to Me 9
CHAPTER TWO
Let Us Offer His Blood Unto Our Gods 29
CHAPTER THREE
You Shall Be Reunited with Your Father 41
CHAPTER FOUR
I Live, But He Lives Not 57
CHAPTER FIVE
I Wish Them Delivered Alive 79
CHAPTER SIX
The Open Sarcophagus of Nerau-Ta 87
CHAPTER SEVEN
I Stand Before You 105
CHAPTER EIGHT
I Have Seen the Stars 115
CHAPTER NINE
If You Do Not Find Him, Ants Will Devour You 139
CHAPTER TEN
And He Was Swallowed By Darkness 149
CHAPTER ELEVEN
The Hands of Priests Stretch to the Ends of the Earth 167

CHAPTER ONE
Ida, Mountain of Our Forefathers, Be Kind to Me

As recently as yesterday, the immortal gods, whose mighty hands grip tightly the veil of the future, refused to reveal to him what events would follow. He had sheltered the night in a desolate shepherd hut in the mountains at the foot of Mount Ida. His mother had sent him to search for herbs at midnight. Some of them bloomed for no longer than a few days and, when properly dried, were used to preserve gutted fish. It was evening when he reached home and entered. His mother was standing in front of the kitchen fire. His father, seated upon some goat skins, slowly lifted his head.

"I am home, mother, and I have brought with me enough herbs for a whole year!"

His mother smiled and nodded but suddenly turned away her saddened face.

His father stood up, lifted the herbs, scrutinized them in the flickering light of the fire, and placed them on a shelf by the wall.

"Did you pick them by night?" his words chimed with natural tranquility, yet Whitehair knew that something was amiss. He looked around the room. Everything was in its place: the goatskins, the crocks, the table, the bench, and the statuette of Great Mother overlooking the doorway.

"Yes, father."

"Have you paid homage to Her?"

"Yes, father."

"By moonlight?"

"Yes, father. The king must have commanded the horses to be driven up north, for as I looked down from the mountain, I caught no sight of them, neither today nor yesterday."

"The early months of summer bring taller grasses to the regions of the north," said his father. "The beauty of Trojan horses cannot be equaled. Only the most luscious grasses will do for them."

Silence fell. His mother indicated the table and placed a crock upon it. He was about to sit down when his father added calmly:

"Yes, they cannot be equaled. The royal herald rode in today on a white stallion. I would give many riches for such a horse—if I had any riches."

"The royal herald, father?"

These were his only words, for he knew it was wrong to question one's father or mother.

"Yes. The king wants to build a new wall around the city, or perhaps he intends to make the present one higher. He will need many helpers. Work might last a month, but I tell you that I might as easily not return until winter. You will remain here with your mother."

"Yes, father." Whitehair sat down and looked at the food, for he was hungry.

Later on, he lay alone at night and listened to the steady breathing of his parents. They were without winter supplies, and if his father departed, he would be forced to go fishing each day, for it was necessary to dry enough fish to satisfy the royal tribute before they could even lay anything by. Never before had he fished alone. His father was yet to take him to the old man on top of the precipice where a cavern led towards a subterranean lake linked to the sea. It was the place where Poseidon retired whilst roaming his domain, and the old man served as his priest. At the time of initiation, the son of each fisherman entered this cavern and bathed his hands in the water of the lake. At times Poseidon revealed himself to the visitor, and perhaps other strange events took place, but Whitehair could only surmise, for never did the initiated speak of what befell them in the depths of the cavern. The tiring journey from the mountains and the fatigue which now filled his body suddenly overwhelmed his mind. He could hardly believe that his father was really going to lead him to the old man after he returned from Troy.

He was roused by the hushed voices of his parents. Opening his eyes, he saw his mother tying a knot in a white cloth bundle while his father, sitting upon a bench, was rubbing oil into his sandal-straps. And presently, his father departed.

Whitehair strained his eyes. A thread of walls and tiny towers running down a distant hillside loomed out of the morning mist. The day was going to be hot, too hot. He looked into the cloudless heavens and, in his mind, repeated what his father had said: "Now, my son, you may. This is the day you have been waiting for, the day on which you shall go fishing on your own. But remember, always keep near the shore. If the heavens grow dark and threatening, waste no time and turn back."

He turned and walked along the winding path which ran between the rocks. From afar, behind the boulder beyond which the hut of his parents stood, he could hear the familiar, muffled, grinding sound of the quern and his mother's soft humming. The tune was always the same: a moiety of lament and laudation: an invocation to Great Mother, the Guardian of life on earth: the Song of the quern. He entered. The quern fell silent, and his mother lifted her eyes.

"Did he let you?" she asked calmly.

Approaching, he took hold of the quern-staff and rotated it softly upon its axis. Once more, the stone began to rattle, and once more, it fell silent.

"You knew I would ask him?"

"Fourteen years have passed since the gods granted you life and filled me with the joy of you. After four and ten winters, your father went fishing on his own, just like his father and mine had done. Yet I thought in my heart that he would send you out alone only after his return. Once the winter is over, you will go with him to the old man in the cavern and there become a man. You are sensible and have some knowledge of the sea. He could not refuse you, for the gods have made their decision. Will you fish today?"

"Yes, mother."

"Then let the Immortals send you fish and fill your heart with joy!"

Whitehair shuddered. As far back as he could remember, she spoke the same words whenever his father went out fishing.

She turned away, quickly wiped a tear from her bashful face, and smiled at him.

"You have grown. You are almost as tall as he is."

She reached for a piece of bread lying beside the fire, stripped it of the large leaf wrapped around it, and gave it to him. He started eating and helped himself to some milk from a two-eared pitcher.

They fell silent, for the graver the matter, the greater the attention of the gods, and no mortal ever knew for sure what could kindle their wrath or fill them with joy. He got up and approached the wall, where he inspected the harpoons and tridents hanging there. The noise of the quern continued, and he could still hear his mother humming, but he knew her eyes were upon him.

There were four harpoons in all: each one a powerful oaken shaft tipped with the straight point of a buffalo horn filled with lead.

Whenever he fished with his father, the lightest one served him well. But this time, he merely weighed it in his hand and replaced it on its peg. Instinctively he turned around. His mother was staring at the stone, feigning indifference to his procedures.

Whitehair took another slightly heavier harpoon and skimmed its blade with his fingertips. Next, he tested the strength of the line passed through the opening at the base of the shaft and, at last, deposited his weapon upon the smaller of two sails, lying folded in the corner of the room. Furtively he placed a hand upon his chest, where, beneath his khiton and tucked away in a sheath of goatskin, he kept his timeless companion—a long-bladed dagger. He reached for the trident, a pruned and blackened branch of oak, forking out into three prongs. Three bits of tunny jaw jutted out of its wooden tips. Each was as sharp as a bronze spearhead. Carefully, Whitehair placed the trident beside the harpoon and removed his khiton so that now he stood only in his tight-fitting loincloth. Leaning forward, he picked up the sail and was ready to depart.

"I am leaving, mother!" Barely had he drawn back the curtain with his shoulder and stood on the threshold when the quern fell silent, and she was at his side.

"A hot morning today," she almost whispered. "Too hot. Watch the heavens, my son, and observe the mountains."

Whitehair nodded.

"Yes, mother. Do not worry."

"And remember, you must pray to the gods."

"That I shall, mother."

He went out. The entire surface of the sea was bathed in gentle sunshine, and the wind had died down completely.

Whitehair descended to the fishing-boats. There were two in all: one large and one small. Having unfastened the smaller one, he directed its stem towards the water and set about slicing it down over the sand. For a whole year now, he had done this on his own. But he could never hope to do the same with the large one. He sighed, pushed the boat, and jumped in.

He attached the tiny sail to the crosswise seat, tied it down, and, lifting the short oar of large outspreading plumes, touched his forehead with its shaft, stood up, and raised his eyes.

"O grant that this boat returns!"

And then the boat floated gracefully onto the water, leaving the coastal rocks with the push of an oar, but the young Trojan rowed for some time steadily, fearing to look back, lest an evil spirit should hinder him upon his homeward journey. His heart was pounding, but not from exertion: never before had he been alone at sea.

Time passed slowly, and Whitehair remained sitting at the

back of the boat. Just in front of him, the drooping sail was rubbing silently against the mast. A dark spine of headland emerged to his left, from where a slight northern wind would push him towards the boundless shallows of the south. It was here that even huge fish could be found wandering close to the surface. Many a time had he visited these vast expanses with his father. But today, he was alone. Be rowed steadily, observing the headland. At last, the contours of an island came into view. It was called Tenedos.

"What would my father do now? From Tenedos, he would make for the shallows and fish at their boundary. But he would return long before sunset, for should a storm arise, his craft would be swept away from the shore by an adverse wind."

And such, indeed, was the case, for, at this time of the year, winds blew from beyond the mountains. If a sudden storm arose, even if the fragile boat were not capsized, it would infallibly be carried out onto the open sea. Even an experienced sailor might never glimpse his native shores again.

Suddenly it crossed his mind that he must return earlier, for a storm could disperse the goats, and if any of them should stray to the fringe of the forest by night, they could easily fall prey to a panther.

Gradually the island emerged from beyond the headland. An agelong forest of oak covered its mountain-side. He had once been to the island with his father. The king of Tenedos was the brother of the Trojan king to whom the entire seacoast and adjacent lands belonged, and it was there that the black warships of both brothers were always guarding access to the city of Troy and the straits leading to the northern sea. It was a formidable fleet, yet at times, by night, a red Phoenician ship or a black fifty-oared vessel of the Achaean corsairs managed to steal its way between the island and the coast and take slaves not far from the city gates. No article of trade was valued more highly or sought for more eagerly than human merchandise.

But during the day, the Trojan waters were safe, and people fished in them without fear. No pirate in the world would venture to draw near the City of Kings in broad daylight.

A breeze drifted over the boat and creased the surface of the sea. A stretch of deep water, dark and green, expanded before his eyes. Somewhat further, the sea appeared to be almost white. This was where the shallows were.

He threaded the harpoon line through the opening at the front of the boat, fastened it firmly, placed the harpoon by his right foot, and reached for the trident. Gripping it with his outstretched arm, he turned to face the shore, but the sun dazzled him and forced him to shade his eyes. He searched out the towering mountaintop looming out of the white haze above a chain of hills.

"Ida, mountain of our forefathers, Great Mother, be kind to me! Behold, now I begin to fish!"

He knitted his brows. No, not a thing had he overlooked. He had uttered all those words a fisherman should utter. And now he turned to look the other way and thought no more of the gods, of the holy mountain, or of his home. Ahead of him were the shallows and in them swam creatures that he would have to slay.

Slowly, as though careful not to startle an invisible fish, he lifted an arm over the side of the boat and, clenching his trident, became motionless.

"I will strike the first one I see. It will be an omen. If I pierce it, my day will be a success."

He waited a long time. Kneeling down, he peered into the water and tried to penetrate the sun-bathed surface. Suddenly, just below him, a small silvery shape flitted by. Instantaneously he struck the water and raised the trident back up. A small fish was struggling, impaled on one of its blades. He lowered his weapon and eased his catch into the bottom of the boat. The fish leaped up high. Whitehair tapped it gently on the head with the shaft of his trident. At once, it stopped moving. A good omen.

He looked up and noticed that he had reached the shallows. The current was sufficiently strong to draw him towards the island.

Once again, a small fish flitted by just below the surface, and it was soon followed by another.

Whitehair placed the trident down and took hold of the harpoon. Shoals of tiny fish were abundant in these waters.

Possibly, if his father were sitting behind him, he would have taken aim yet again and made a show of his dexterity. But today, he was alone. If the omen was correct, fate would lead him to a greater catch. So he gripped the heavy harpoon-shaft and waited. Suddenly his fingers tightened around the weapon. Some distance off, a tiny fish shot up into the air and, flashing brilliantly in the sun, vanished into the depths again. Closer still, he noticed another fish. And in no time at all, an incessant swarm of scudding, nimble, fleeting flashes surrounded the boat. An enormous shoal of fish was passing with blind impetus, brushing against the tiny vessel and rushing on just below the surface.

They were terrified. And now they fled to the center of the shallows. Watching as they approached in their thousands, he tried to understand what was happening. If the assailant of this panic-stricken shoal was advancing deep down, he would soon be forced to reveal himself as the sea bed rose abruptly under his belly.

The surface was lifeless. But suddenly—yes! He managed to catch a glimpse of the pursuer just before he plunged again: a huge, sharp fin of an enormous fish. Presently two more emerged, a little to the right. Tunnies!

Huge and voracious, these oppressors had probably encountered this shoal of placid fish quite recently and were presently tracking it down, seizing victims, devouring them instantaneously, and charging on.

"You have come!" He whispered. "You have come!"

These were the largest of fish in these waters, apart from dolphins, which were sacred and which no one ever dared to strike. They gave suck to their young, and therefore, they could well have once been an ancient tribe of men sentenced by the gods to dwell in the waters for evil deeds committed in days of yore.

But a tunny was the most magnificent of catches, a creature that rarely lost a fight. The largest of these exceeded the length of a fishing boat, and only a very experienced fisherman could be a match for them. Their strength was colossal, and failure to slay one with a single blow of a harpoon—which had to enter between their side fin and the gills and pierce their heart—could mean the loss of the weapon, or the vessel, or even of one's life because the injured fish would whip its enormous tail about in savage agony and could shatter a tiny boat with ease.

Once again, the long, cerulean fin of a tunny appeared before him, far closer now and then, once again, closer still. Then, momentarily, the fish emerged nearly entirely and vanished, plunging after its prey.

Whitehair looked about eagerly. He had almost reached the center of the shallows. If the tunnies continued their pursuit, they would soon appear just below the surface.

Slowly the seabed drew closer and closer, and peering down, he noticed dark seaweed and white sand illuminated by the rays of the sun.

As far back as he could remember, he had always bathed here, and it was here that he had learned to swim. He felt completely safe in the water, safer in fact than on land, for land undoubtedly harbored greater dangers than the sea. He was well aware that this stretch of water was no deeper than the height of three grown men.

A tunny, if found here within striking distance of a harpoon, would have no chance of escaping into deeper waters, for with its body dreadfully torn, it would be forced to push forward with the boat in tow until its strength was gone.

He knew this from his father, who had smitten and slain three tunnies in a single day in this place.

Again he saw the blade of a fin beating the water into a white spray. The tunnies drew away somewhat, still circling around the boat.

They were now in the center of the fleeing shoal, and they slowed down. They kept breaking the surface: one... two... three... four... he spotted four in all. One of them was no further away than just a few spear throws, but suddenly they all swung round and started making for the island.

He sighed and watched them disappear. He had not really believed that the immortal gods might have offered him such a magnificent gift. And yet—they had been so close!

Again, he sighed as they dissolved in the flickering surface, and now he observed the water stretching in front of him.

A few small fish slipped past quickly and scattered in all directions. Undoubtedly the hounded shoal had dispersed, or maybe it was still heading towards the island but had lost this panic-stricken group which now sought to rejoin its companions. There were certain kinds of fish who never traveled alone but always as whole nations. Did such nations have their kings?

He put the harpoon away and took hold of the trident, for he wished to return home with a laden boat. Once again, fish started appearing in greater numbers. They ripped through the water much faster now, all of them in the same direction. Before long, there was a swarm of them. The shoal was returning!

Again he caught sight of a long, white streak of splashing water, plowed with astonishing speed by the dark blade of a fin. Then another, and still one more. The tunnies were coming back!

They were only a short distance away. One had outdistanced the rest. Whitehair seized the harpoon and raised it over his head.

Swimming just below the surface and leaving a bright trail, the tunny approached the boat and, changing direction, encircled it with a wide curve before dissolving in the reflections of the sun. A second and a third one passed by at some distance and pushed on in the same direction. He followed them with his eyes as far as the boundary of the shallows.

Only now did he realize that he had been standing motionless for some time, holding his harpoon above his head. He lowered his weapon. It was time for him to catch as many small fish as possible and return home. Maybe before sunset, some bigger fish would reappear.

He knew that the tunnies would not return the following day, for never did they dwell in any one place for too long. Often he had heard his father say that they wandered from one end of the world to the next and, having reached it, turned round to head back again. These must have just returned from the other side of the sea. Perhaps they may want to bide their time and rest a little after their long journey?

Reluctantly, he looked at the water in front of the boat and thought it a good idea to practice a little by tossing his harpoon at a few passing fish.

And suddenly he saw it!

Just below the surface, to the left of the stem, a huge tunny had stopped. It seemed to be contemplating the boat as though confused by the presence of this piece of wood and the towering creature standing on it and staring at it.

Time stopped. The whole world suddenly vanished. Unconscious of his actions, Whitehair lifted his harpoon and hurled it with all his might.

He watched as the line chased after the harpoon. The harpoon entered the water and struck the creature near the semicircular opening of its gills, where its sky-blue back and its white belly-line merged, right next to the enormous side fin, sharp as a dagger and long as an arm.

Suddenly, he was swept off his feet by a colossal jolt that jerked his boat. He shot up into the air and fell into the water on the opposite side of the boat.

Now the sky disappeared, and a bluish-green glow of tarnished sunrays enveloped him. For a moment, he fell in stupefaction: instinctively waving his arms about, he saw the water surface closing in on him.

Emerging, he looked about for his boat, which, to his great astonishment, was so far away that a great fear gripped his heart. How could it have moved away so quickly?

Desperately pushing through the water, he began pursuing

his vessel. An enormous, invisible power jerked the boat along, slowing down, speeding up, and at times even stopping.

"The line is strong," he thought. "I have smitten him..."

But instantly, he realized that the tunny was still alive. The harpoon was undoubtedly embedded deep in its side, for otherwise, the injured fish would have torn itself loose easily. But what if it had enough strength to swim into the distance, carrying his tiny craft away?

He did not look at the shore, for he was well aware of how far the rocky headland was. Maybe he could manage to swim back? But then the boat would be lost, and he would not be able to fish anymore until his father returned in winter. This could not happen, for everyone would then go hungry, and shame would descend upon him for having lost the boat—and that on the very first day he fished alone.

Now the boat stopped moving. Maybe the tunny was resting, trying to regain strength? The wound and the additional weight of the boat may have exhausted him.

Whitehair reached for his dagger dangling from his neck and drew it out of its sheath. The boat was now right in front of him.

Taking a deep breath and moving with the utmost care, he dove under it and emerged on the other side, in the shadow of the boat. He rested his palm gently against the edge of its stem and breathed heavily for some time. His right hand was clenching the dagger.

Slowly he submerged his head and, looking about with open eyes, observed the line running down from the stem and fading amongst the lawn of seaweeds at the bottom, twining up towards the surface. A huge, dark, distant shape loomed amongst them.

Once again, he lifted his head out of the water, inhaled as much air as possible, and dove down.

Easing his way through the seaweed, he moved slowly and with extreme care, keeping close to the bottom. He tried to follow the direction of the line which he could see overhead.

He stopped. The fish was right in front of him. It was floating on one side, sagging a little so that its head and tail were lower than its middle. Streaks of blood poured from its left side and slowly twisted their way up, imitating the undulating flow of seaweeds.

The fish was enormous! Almost twice his own size! Only the end of the harpoon shaft protruded from the wound. The flesh beneath its side-fin had been pierced, this being the exact place where a harpoon should be lodged if, as his father had told him so many times, the king of the sea was to perish.

But had it perished? It remained completely still, swaying gently in the current, yet this did not mean that it was lifeless.

Whitehair felt the air escaping from his lungs and swam to the surface. He breathed in deeply, closed his eyes, dazzled by the sunlight, and plunged back down immediately.

Passing the fish and moving along near the bottom, he turned on to his back and faced the distant sky above. Now he approached the tunny from below, gripped his dagger with both hands, and with a sudden kicking action with his legs, pushed himself up.

Now, clinging to the white and scaly body of the giant, he drove his dagger in deep and tore away at it with all his might. The flesh submitted easily to the merciless blade.

At once, he curled up and plunged straight down, touching the bottom. But the tremendous toss of the body and the violent flap of the tail that he had expected did not follow. He looked up.

The fish swayed passively, and a fresh stream of blood burst forth from its huge new wound.

"I slew him with a single blow," thought Whitehair. "I struck his heart and killed him!"

One again, he came to the surface and looked at the distant shore, bathed in blazing sunshine. "This winter, when they take me to the old man, Father will speak of my catch, and together we shall lay the head of the beast at the foot of the cavern."

He was so filled with joy that he remained upon the surface for a little while longer. But he now thought of the vast amount of work ahead of him and returned to the lifeless giant.

He swam up to its muzzle, forced it open, and carving a hole in its lower jaw, pushed through the harpoon and line, and tied a knot so as to lean the harpoon shaft against its head.

Once more, he came to the surface. And only now did he realize how exhausted he really was, for much of his strength was gone, and with a thundering heart, he scrambled onto the boat.

He took a deep breath. Battling with his fatigue—for he was tempted to sink to the bottom of the boat and rest awhile—he started tugging the line. It yielded with difficulty, and he could not be sure whether the tunny was drawing closer or the boat approaching the lifeless form. His hands had grown numb. But gradually, pull after pull, the line gathered in a coil at his feet.

And at last, leaning over the water, he perceived it. The tunny slipped alongside the boat and rolled over onto its back. Its tail remained submerged.

Whitehair secured the line, slipped down onto his knees, and leaned his back against the mast. Sweat streamed down his face, and only a flogging could have matched the agonizing pain which ran through his shoulders. He closed his eyes and breathed in deeply, but still, he found it difficult to gather his thoughts. Nonetheless, his half-closed, parched lips constantly repeated:

"I must chop it into large pieces... chop it up and take as much meat as I can... and the head... the head... I can never reach the shore with this body in one piece... Mother will fill the head with herbs... dry it in the sun... Then we shall take it..."

He opened his eyes and stood up heavily. His heart was no longer pounding, but the pain in his back persisted.

He glanced at the spot where the line touched the water. The gentle waves had rolled the tunny over so that it now floated on the surface, its body drooping slightly but its head up high. Its lifeless eyes, almost as blue as the sky itself, gazed blindly into the heavens.

There was no more blood coming from its wounds, and the water about the boat started losing its red tinge. Whitehair reached for his dagger and dove out of the boat.

Gritting his teeth, he toiled over his prey and sliced sizeable chunks of pinkish-white flesh, injuring his fingers upon its enormous bones and rock-hard fins. At last, he was ready.

The head had come off with great difficulty and now rocked a little, for it was still held by the line passed through the hole in its lower jaw.

At once, he unfastened the line and swam towards the boat. With difficulty, he lifted the gigantic head and tossed it upon the huge slices of the gory flesh scattered about the bottom of the boat—the boat deeply submerged now, hardly rocking under all the weight.

So wearied was he that he sprawled on the cool, slippery, slithering slices of flesh for a while. Presently he rose and, having taken in the sail, took hold of the oar.

A light breeze blew straight into his eyes. He turned the boat around towards the headland, which appeared to be quite close but, in reality, was much further away. Beyond the headland was his native shore and his mother, who would be awaiting his return. She would see him from afar and descend towards the water, curious to see his catch. And when this monstrous muzzle met her eye...

He broke out of his daydream rather abruptly and looked at the creature's head lying upon the slices of flesh near the bow of the boat. Quickly dropping his oar, he leaned towards the harpoon, picked it up, and with all his might, pierced the jaw of the tunny, nailing its huge head to the bottom of the boat. Next, he pulled the harpoon line through the aperture at the stem and secured it tightly. No unexpected wave or sudden jolt could now snatch his prize away.

Gradually he started rowing and tried to hum to himself. But so wearied was he that at once he fell silent. He observed the headland as it gradually moved past and awaited the appearance of his native shore.

The sun no longer dazzled his eyes. It had wandered across

the heavens towards setting.

"I could almost match a true man, despite my age!" he cried out. "No fisherman would venture to pronounce the solitary slayer of a tunny a mere boy."

The headland fell away to his right, and the distant shore opened up before his eyes, unfolding with every stroke of his oar.

In a moment, the hilltop would emerge, followed by the thickets and the huge, white boulder resting beside a low, rocky slope, and not far from the boulder...

He put more effort into his rowing, still more... and beheld a remote, white speck. The boulder and beyond it: his house!

Ceasing the rowing for a while, he rose and lifted his eyes towards the distant summit of the holy mountain, dominating the entire landscape, and opened his mouth, ready to pronounce unto the gods words of thanksgiving, for they had guided him on his hunt and permitted him to return with a good catch.

But his prayer was imprisoned on his tongue. The mountain, he now realized, had taken on a new shape, for just above its summit, he perceived yet another summit, darker and somewhat rounded.

"A cloud?" the thought ran through his mind, and at that moment, a flash appeared before his eyes, blinding white and sharp. So intense was it that even the brilliant sunshine failed to extinguish it.

He froze. A few seconds passed, then a muffled, rumbling clap of thunder reached him from a distance. The sea was calm, and there was no wind.

"Mother!" whispered Whitehair. Overcoming his sudden, heart-gripping fear, he snatched up the oar. "Row calmly," he said to himself aloud, "calmly, if you wish to save your strength and return to shore."

Unable to take his eyes off the black cloud emerging above the mountains, he rowed desperately, filled with terror, and his burdened boat crept along slowly, extremely slowly, in the dead silence which had seized the sea and air.

The cloud grew and spilled over the land. And the restless rays of the sun seemed to burn even more.

Whitehair rested his oar for a while and wiped away the sweat streaming down his forehead and into his eyes, making it impossible to see.

The shore drew closer. He could clearly see the familiar outline of the rocks and the contours of mountains, which would shortly be embraced by the murky shadow of the approaching storm.

Undoubtedly his mother was waiting there and could see him. She would be aware of his solitary battle with the still, tranquil water but would have no idea why the boat was so heavy.

"If I throw some of the meat into the sea, I shall make it," he thought in a flash.

But he knew this was not true, for already the cloud had swallowed the mountain and blanketed the entire horizon to the east. To throw tunny meat away would have meant wasting time... too much time.

A slight breath of wind whispered in the air.

Another flash, bloody in color, appeared upon the fringe of the cloud, and this was followed by a tremendous, shrill peal of thunder that roared across the sea with the sound of shattering wood.

Now a different thought entered his mind: "It will be quicker to swim. Then I shall be saved!" But he hesitated and continued to row with what strength he had.

And then he saw her. There she was, standing beside the water, a mere speck in the distance, growing closer, waving her upraised arms and giving him courage—his mother!

No, he could not jump, for if the storm hit the sea before he reached the shore, he would be too weak to oppose the oncoming, billowing waves, whereas the boat offered him at least a shadow of hope.

Suddenly the sun disappeared, and now the sea was filled with gloom. A gust of wind hit him.

He could still see his mother when the first large wave

approached and hit the boat head-on.

Another thunderclap yet again. And then the chain of hills disappeared from view. Too late. Another wave approached, crashed down, and he felt the boat retreating. With an enormous effort, he dipped his oar again, and this cost him the whole of his might. The shore and everything around him plunged into darkness. In the midst of the roaring murkiness, streams of rain lashed across his face, and he fell to the bottom of the boat, covering his head with his hands.

The boat rocked, leaped into the air, riding the crest of the oncoming wave, descended, and once again seized by some unseen force, jumped up and tilted over violently.

Blindly he gripped the loosely lying line of the harpoon, which was firmly lodged in the side of the boat and hardly aware of his actions, wrapped it around his left wrist and grasped it with both hands.

He could feel the boat rising and sinking. A huge wave rolled over his head, choking him and sweeping large pieces of tunny away.

The storm wailed on incessantly.

Lying in the bottom and attempting to catch as much air as possible before the descent of the next huge wave, Whitehair knew just one thing for sure: that the storm and wind were propelling his tiny vessel out onto the open sea, leaving his native shores farther and farther behind.

CHAPTER TWO
Let Us Offer His Blood Unto Our Gods

The sun set in blood-red glory, leaving the sea silent and dark, but its rays still illuminated the few remaining scraps of black clouds which rushed southwards in pursuit of the retreating storm.

Most venerable Ahikar looked at the badly damaged mast and shreds of purple sail, swaying to and fro as his ship gradually rocked along. The bronze bust of Asherah, Our Lady of the Seas, which graced the towering, curved prow of the ship, plunged into the water and heaved itself back into view again. Though the sea remained perturbed and billowy, a soothing peace began to prevail.

Staggering, Ahikar approached the side of the ship and observed the flickering dance of sparkling waves. His lips moved silently as he counted the oars. He hated rough seas, and if ever he decided to tell his crew the truth about himself, he would tell them that he hated calm seas also.

Whenever he sailed, he was ill and nauseous, and only thanks to the herbs of Gubal did he feel any better, but these herbs had to be drunk hot a few times each day, and already much time had passed since one of his men had last kindled a fire in the small stone hearth at the stern.

Indeed, so awe-stricken had he been during the storm that all thought of suffering had escaped his mind. And when the upper part of the mast crashed down, and the quickly taken-in sail ripped into shreds, and a huge wave descended upon the oars, smashing two of them away and killing one of his rowers –an unfortunate victim of the merciless blow of his tool - Ahikar became convinced that the hand of fate had fallen on his ship and on his own life as well.

His crew had wailed with fear as water gushed over the side whilst he, Ahikar, master of twenty ships and the largest stores in Gubal, stood tied down to the foot of the mast—having ordered his men to tie him there —and awaited his end. He did not believe in the almighty gods and, at that moment, regretted it bitterly, for he knew that his oarsmen and captain were invoking the help of Asherah, Our Lady of the Seas, promising Her the costliest offerings if only She delivered their ship from the danger it faced.

Now he smiled and stroked his beard. Though he was an old man, he loved life as much as anyone. Nevertheless, despite the raging storm, he had faced death bravely, knowing well that it must visit him one day. It could well have arrived now, but it did not. The wild tempest had spared the vessel, which now crawled along heading south, towards home.

And again, Ahikar stroked his beard. Then he held his hand up to his face and sighed deeply. In the morning, his beard had still been crimson and beautifully curled. But now, much of the dye had vanished, and in many places, patches of grey began to show. However, at present other things were of greater importance, and therefore, he did not ask for the mirror, which was always kept in his chest in the hold.

Ahikar smiled again. His audience with the king of Troy had been a success. He would need the help of middlemen no more. From now on, his own ships would provide the Pharaoh with Trojan silver, and in return, Phoenicia would furnish Troy lavishly with the pick of her riches: splendid tapestries and glassware as could be found nowhere else in the world.

Through the corner of his eye, he noticed the captain who was standing with his head lowered and arms crossed over his chest.

"Why, Tabnit! I read fear in your eyes. Do you expect another storm, or has this last one, through anxiety, sealed your lips?"

"No, master!" The captain approached and lowered his head even more. "Baal has passed thunderously upon his mighty course and will undoubtedly not return for long. We may be sure of a calm sea and a favorable wind for some days now. Praise and glory to the shipwrights of Sidon! Never before have I sailed upon a better ship, though it is the merciful gods we should thank, for, without them, our bones would be resting at the bottom of the sea. We must pay homage to them."

"True, true..." Ahikar nodded. "Indeed, the gods have shown us kindness. Therefore we shall make a splendid offering of many goats upon the altar of Our Lady of the Seas as soon as we reach home. And here," he indicated a flat stone surrounded by a cedar frame, set just behind a carved likeness of the goddess, "you will burn these fragrances as soon as they are dry, for water appears to have penetrated everywhere."

"Yes, master. It shall be done."

"Well, now. Tell me, Tabnit, how far have we to sail?"

"As soon as the sea is calm, the shipwright will repair the mast. Then we shall see to making a new spar and fitting the spare sail to it. Two men are adjusting it already. The oars are also being repaired, but a good wind would help us greatly."

"If the gods grant it..." breathed Ahikar and smiled, knowing that his beard was masking his face.

"Yes, master. Should I kindle a fire and prepare the fragrances for the altar?"

"This you must do at once, for we have nothing else to offer. And remember, the crew must be nourished, and my herbs must be prepared!"

"Yes, master!"

The captain stepped back.

Ahikar approached the side of the ship and gazed across the sea. He could hear the captain issuing commands in a loud, harsh voice. The sound of axes and hammers echoed throughout the ship. It was the shipwrights making critical repairs.

31

The old man sighed.

"I am wealthy," he thought. "Why do I wander so far and wide in search of even greater riches when any of my sons could easily take my place?"

But at once, he answered himself.

"They are young and foolish. The king of Troy would wind them around his thumb. And as for my younger son, it is enough to treat him with greater familiarity than is usual at a feast where the wine is good, and at once, he will think himself amongst friends and will be ready to buy silver adulterated with lead."

He smiled.

"However, I shall wander the seas no more... or maybe, maybe just once more, to Egypt, for I must draw this last enterprise of mine to a successful close..."

Still thinking, he looked at the waves, which no longer rose in a foamy spray. The sun was setting, and still, Ahikar looked down in thought. Suddenly he lifted his head and turned around.

"Tabnit!"

The captain appeared above the wooden staircase leading down towards the thwarts.

"Yes, master! Did you call me?"

"Come closer and look yourself. I have the eyes of an old man and am probably mistaken, thinking I caught a glimpse of something. But tell me, do you see a boat blowing in the wind? Look, yonder?" And he pointed with his arm.

The captain nodded.

"Yes, master! There is a boat. The storm must have driven it here."

"Is it empty? My sight tells me someone is in it."

"Indeed, master, there is someone in it."

"Then we must check, Tabnit, whether this mortal still breathes or whether he has perished in the storm."

Quickly the captain reached the staircase and shouted a command. At once, the oars rose out of the water and froze in the air.

"Hamman!" called the captain.

Presently the figure of a tall, dark-haired oarsman drew near. He fell to his knees and rose at once.

"Do you see that boat? You must jump into the water and tell me what you find there. I see a man. If he is alive, bring him here."

Without a word, the swarthy slave ran up to the side of the ship and made a powerful dive into the sea, clearing the oars hovering over the water and vanishing in the waves. He reappeared immediately, and everyone observed him attentively. He soon leaned on the stem of the tiny boat, pulled himself up, and peered in.

"A boy, master!" sounded his voice. "A boy, tied to the boat! He cannot possibly be alive!"

The captain hesitated and looked at Ahikar.

"Let him be sure of his words."

"Press your ear against his chest!" shouted the captain.

The oarsman slipped into the boat, lifted the limp body, and, kneeling down, listened for the sound of life. Presently he rose.

"He is alive. I hear the voice of his heart."

"Let him come nearer with the boat," murmured Ahikar, "for I wish to inspect it."

The boy undoubtedly was an inhabitant of the Troad. It was important to understand and learn about the people with whom one exchanged goods.

The captain shouted an order to his crew down below. And presently, he was given a long line which he gripped by one end and hurled overboard. The swarthy oarsman caught it in the air. At last the small boat and the slender, motionless body found themselves upon the deck. Ahikar approached and scrutinized the boy, who moved his head a little, opened his eyes briefly, and closed them again.

"The People of the Sea who dwell beyond the Trojan inlet have children whose hair is as fair as his, or maybe this mortal has even fairer hair," he appeared to be murmuring to himself and the captain.

"Yes, master," answered Tabnit and fell silent.

Ahikar walked up to the boat,

"What does this mean? The head of a tunny with its jaws pierced? Could he have secured it there in order to ward off evil powers?"

The captain came forward and touched the enormous head. With some difficulty, he tore out the harpoon.

"No, master. He must have caught this fish not long ago. Probably no later than midday."

"He?" uttered Ahikar looking at the slender body yet again. "Indeed, he must be a worthy fisherman if, at such a young age, he is capable of hunting down a creature, which with a single stroke of its tail could easily have wiped him and his tiny craft from the surface of the waters. Surely he was accompanied by another, grown man who perished in the storm."

The young Trojan opened his eyes, closed them, and opened them again. In wonder, he stared at the two bearded figures standing over him and attempted to lift himself onto his elbow.

"Tabnit, you speak their tongue. Ask him about the fish."

"Yes, master."

The captain looked at the boy and uttered a few words which Ahikar did not understand. The young Trojan seemed not to understand him. He sat up and slowly touched his forehead. Later, as though suddenly remembering, he looked about and, noticing his vessel close by, kneeled and embraced its side. A great weakness had clearly descended upon him. Looking at the captain, he mumbled something and slumped back onto the deck.

"Yes, master. He was alone and slew the fish himself."

"A true fisherman and a brave man and yet—a mere boy..."

Ahikar nodded and stroked his beard.

"Master..." the captain almost whispered.

For a long time, the old merchant remained silent; then he looked towards the captain:

"Speak, Tabnit."

"Master, will you grant that your most humble servant speak what is on his mind?"

Ahikar nodded assent.

"When your keen eyes, master, spotted the boat and the boy upon the waters, a voice spoke to me from the inside and told me that the merciful gods had bestowed a gift upon us so that we may celebrate our salvation..."

"What do you mean, Tabnit?"

"Master, if you will allow me to continue, then I mean to say that if, after such an awesome storm on the boundless and lonely expanses of the sea, the gods have sent us this castaway, unharmed and away from the fatal jaws of predacious fish, then surely they wish us to sacrifice him on the altar of Asherah, Our Lady of the Seas, to whom we owe our survival."

Ahikar looked at the young Trojan, who sat up, shook his head, and lifted his arms, stretching them out. The glow of the setting sun gleamed on his skin which tightened around his supple, muscular shoulders.

"And, if I may continue, master, it will be a mistake of the gravest kind to oppose the gods who have sent us this omen, for they may become wrathful while we are still on this ship so badly damaged during the storm."

The merchant raised his head in a calm, carefree manner.

"Maybe, Tabnit. Maybe you are right when you speak of making an offering to the gods," he paused and stroked his beard.

"Yes, master! I thank you! Let his blood be offered up to the gods!"

Ahikar barely raised his hand, and the captain immediately fell silent.

"Yes, you are right when you speak of making an offering to the gods. But look here, there is a dagger in a leather sheath dangling upon his neck. And now a voice tells me that by sending me this fisherman, the gods might have signaled me to take hold of his

35

dagger—which has crossed the sea—and make an offering of the man who defeated the same sea by captaining my ship so gallantly through the storm. I mean... make an offering of you, Tabnit. Tell me, which offering would be better? This vile, barbarian stripling? Or you, a fully grown man and dedicated to the sea from childhood?"

He did not raise his voice when he spoke, nor did he alter his gentle tone. But the captain prostrated himself in front of him and embraced his legs, calling:

"Master, do you really intend to sacrifice me?"

"No!" Ahikar shook his head. "You are too brave and too loyal a captain for that. I am sure that Asherah, Our Lady of the Seas, would not desire your blood any more than she desires the blood of this boy here. Rise."

The captain rose to his knees and then, looking into the eyes of the old man, heaved himself onto his feet.

"Could you have forgotten, Tabnit, that I am the wealthiest merchant of Gubal? Could you have forgotten that our king has a brother who is married to my niece? Could you also have forgotten who you are? Have you not been taught in your youth and childhood that never in the presence of your superior will you dare to speak your mind unasked?"

"Master..." the captain barely moved his pale lips. "I beg your forgiveness. The storm has confused my mind, and I am wearied..."

"Indeed," spoke Ahikar calmly. "But take care it does not happen again."

"Have my despicable skin flogged, master, until my blood flows in streams."

"No, Tabnit. Never before have I had the occasion to complain about you. And your family has served mine well for the past two generations. But what do you think our king would say if I ventured to offer him advice without being asked to do so?"

And again, the captain fell to his knees and kissed his master's sandals.

"I swear that the gods and your good fortune have always

been foremost in my mind."

"I believe it," answered Ahikar curtly. "Rise!"

The captain rose again.

"Nourish the boy and be sure that by the time we touch land, he is in good health and fully rested."

"Yes, master."

"And tonight we shall burn this boat of his on the altar of Asherah, Our Lady of the Seas. And the head of this creature along with it."

He looked into the heavens.

"There is a full moon tonight, and our sacrifice will gladden our goddess. Tell the crew that no one is to beat the boy. If I see so much as a single mark on his body, you shall perish, and the one who struck him shall perish with you."

"Yes, master."

"Very well. Go now and prepare my herbs, and if there should be a shred of dry cloth about, prepare it for me to put on. At midnight you shall wake me in time for the sacrifice."

"Yes, master."

With the greatest care, the captain bent down towards the boy, who rose with difficulty and staggered towards the stairs leading down to the oarsmen and the back of the ship.

The old merchant smiled and stroked his beard.

CHAPTER THREE
You Shall Be Reunited with Your Father

Whitehair was sitting on the warm, dry sand. Shaded by the ship, he watched its men busily transporting ashore bales of purple cloth wrapped in white canvas, which had been loaded some twenty days earlier in Gubal.

Ten ships, each with a stem both towering and curved, had entered the mouth of the river at daybreak. Four of them had been towing rafts containing beautifully hewn cedar logs tied securely by bast-fibers. Each of those ships had twice the usual number of oarsmen who took turns to row so as to keep up with the rest of the fleet.

Ahikar called this land Egypt.

Bored with watching the workers, Whitehair now studied Ahikar, who stood apart talking to a tall man dressed in white, undoubtedly someone of great importance, for there was a slave shading his shaven head with a small piece of linen stretched out upon two slender staffs. Some distance behind the tall Egyptian there stood a group of people who had arrived with him: his retinue.

Suddenly Ahikar turned round and indicated Whitehair.

"Undoubtedly, he is explaining how I was found at sea," thought Whitehair and looked towards the city stretching forth to the right of the palm grove. The colossal form of a white palace, bathed in brilliant sunlight, dominated the landscape.

Whitehair stood up and walked across to where the sailors

were depositing the merchandise. A half-naked old man, his legs crossed, was sitting in front of a small, portable table with a wooden stand of cups filled up to the top with thick, dark liquid and a few long, thin writing reeds. Each time a bale of cloth appeared, the old man dipped his writing-reed into the liquid and scratched a sign on the scroll, which had been unfurled and pressed down flat by tiny white stones.

The young Trojan watched him for a while, then walked on. He was strictly forbidden to wander too far from the ship, so he sat down again, facing the distant city.

He thought of Gubal, where he had spent the last few months. On arrival there, he believed it to be the largest city in the world, much larger than his tiny, native Troy.

But nowhere in Gubal was there a temple quite so magnificent as the one he saw now.

He sighed and stood up again. For some time now, he had been suffering from sleeplessness. Because he was forbidden to work, he could not even help the sailors, who were now carefully unloading the long-necked vessels of wine sealed with wax.

His situation puzzled him greatly, for in Gubal, too, it had been the same: he had not been allowed to work, or go swimming, or walk too far from Ahikar's house unless he was accompanied.

As time went on, he resigned himself to his fate, realizing that he was neither the first nor indeed the last man in the world torn away from his fatherland. The house of Ahikar and the entire city of Gubal were full of slaves who had been captured in various parts of the world. They worked hard from dawn till dusk, and though some of them, such as the ones skilled in arts and crafts, wore beautiful robes and lived in abundance, their lives were always in the hands of their master.

But of all the fates of captives in Gubal, his fate was undoubtedly the strangest. No sooner had they touched land than the old merchant entrusted him to the care of a trusted slave, who followed him about everywhere like a shadow.

His only pastime was a leisurely stroll around the city. Soon he grew accustomed to staring eyes. Even in Troy, it was difficult to find someone with fairer skin and whiter hair, and here, where people were much darker than in the north, everyone was filled with surprise.

And thus, his time passed in Gubal. Each day the slave applied an ointment to his skin and checked his body with the greatest care, looking for scratches and blemishes. When, after some time, he learned the Phoenician tongue a little, he asked the slave the reason for this, and he, answering in the words of his master, said:

"His body must be spotless."

And at last, the day arrived when Ahikar called him to himself and ordered him to stand naked with his loincloth in his hand.

After a short inspection, the merchant nodded silently and indicated the door, clearly pleased with what he had seen.

On the following day, just before daybreak, the old slave woke Whitehair from his sleep.

"Rise! Today our master is taking you to Egypt. May Baal prolong his life for many years to come!"

And so Whitehair washed himself in the garden by the cistern and hanged his dagger in its goatskin sheath about his neck. This was his only possession and his only reminder of his former life.

And then the slave escorted him to the port where the ships were already awaiting, ready for departure.

And so here he was, resting upon the shore of this strange land called Egypt, lazily observing the large vessels of wine standing in a row and the pile of bales of purple cloth dyed so nobly in Gubal by the slaves of Ahikar.

"O Son of the Waters!"

Quickly, he turned around. It was the old merchant who always used these playful words when addressing him. But today, his face was grave. His tall Egyptian companion, a long, golden-handled staff in his left hand, bid him approach.

Whitehair came closer and bowed before Ahikar. And when the Egyptian came up to him and, stretching forth his arm, loosened his loincloth so that it fell onto the ground, he did not stir.

He noticed that the people standing behind the Egyptian were craning their necks to get a better view of him, whilst some of them had taken a step forward.

The scribe who had been entering the merchandise in the long scroll raised his hand, forbidding anyone else to leave the ship.

Absolute silence prevailed as the tall Egyptian slowly walked around Whitehair. His large, steady eyes rolled over the boy's slender body.

Having at last finished the inspection, he stepped aside and, turning towards the people standing behind him, uttered a few incomprehensible words. One of the men bowed solemnly. They exchanged a few words, and then the one who had bowed approached the young Trojan.

"Where are you from, and how is it you belong to Ahikar, the merchant of Gubal? Speak, for my master, Het-Ka-Sebek, Priest of the Temple of the God Who Dwells in the Waters, awaits your answer."

His speech was understandable, though it differed somewhat from the tongue used by the fishermen of the Troad coast.

"I am the son of a fisherman," said Whitehair softly. "And my sovereign is the king of Troy."

He was surprised to hear the sound of his own words. Such a long time had passed since he had last used the tongue of his forefathers that he answered with considerable difficulty. But presently, words came to him with greater ease. "I caught a tunny, and as I was struggling with it, a storm arose, and Great Mother, Guardian of Land and Sea, chose to send a violent wind which threw my vessel out to the open sea. Without a breath of life in me, I lay in the boat, and the most venerable Ahikar spotted me amid the waves and ordered his men to bring me on board. Since then, I have lived in his house, and today at sunrise, we arrived here on one of his ships."

"And what is it that your Great Mother and Guardian holds in her hand when you make an image of her in clay or stone?" asked the other man quickly.

"Why, either doves or serpents," answered Whitehair without hesitation. The one who had spoken to him did not await further explanations, for he was already bowing down humbly with arms crossed over his chest and talking hastily to the tall Egyptian. And now that he had finished speaking, a dead silence prevailed. Instinctively Whitehair bent down to pick up his loincloth, but the tall Egyptian threw it aside with the end of his staff. Then, indicating the boy once more, he uttered something and looked at Ahikar.

The old merchant stroked his beard and answered in a few words. Again the tall Egyptian signaled the one standing beside the boy.

"Is this your dagger?"

"Yes," the young Trojan touched his chest, bared his weapon, and inserted it back into its sheath.

"Did you have it with you when the merchant, Ahikar, took you onto his ship?"

"Yes."

The man turned around and, keeping his hands crossed over his chest, repeated what he had heard.

The tall Egyptian spoke to Ahikar.

Now, if Whitehair could have unveiled the secret of his words, he would not have remained there standing patiently and considering the golden staff, whose handle was graced by the jaws of some unknown creature. But as it was, standing with head lowered, he looked at it attentively. Its long and slightly open jaws were full of minute, golden teeth. The sun produced a cold, celestial brilliance that shone brightly out of its tiny eyes. They were made of two precious stones as blue as the sky, the like of which he had never seen before.

In the meantime, the tall Egyptian was saying:

"You have done well, Ahikar, by remembering the many

long-lasting bonds of honest exchange and service which your house has rendered to the God Who Rules in the Great Lake. As you know, my god is most pleased when, on his feast day, he receives those who are without a blemish and whose bodies have emerged out of the waters."

"Yes, Het-Ka-Sebek, Guardian of the Living Effigy of the Soul of Sebek, the god, I have always kept this foremost in mind. And barely had I caught a glimpse of him, his boat dancing upon the billowy sea, and noticed that his body was flawless and without the slightest mark, and his limbs perfectly shaped, but I thought of your great god—O may he bring joy and health to you for thousands of years to come!

"Some of my people wished to offer him up to Our Lady of the Seas, but I would not have it and rebuked them for it. In Gubal, I entrusted him to the care of a loyal slave, who nourished him and applied ointment to his skin so that his appearance would gladden your god. And so he must delight you also, for he is no ordinary boy. His hair is as white as the head of an aged man, though he is still young. A merchant of so many years of experience, could I ever think of damaging such a rare treasure?"

And now Het-Ka-Sebek, Priest and Peace Guardian of the Living Effigy of the Soul of Sebek, the god, bowed his head.

"Yes, Ahikar, you have certainly done the right thing..."

He paused and observed the naked Trojan before them.

"How can my Temple repay you for this service?"

Ahikar stroked his board and cleared his throat.

"Need I remind you, Het-Ka-Sebek, Guardian of the Living Effigy of the Soul of God, that as soon as my ship put in at Gubal with the boy on board, I acknowledged it as something of great importance to inform you at once of his arrival, by sending word through the first vessel leaving for Egypt, that we, the boy and I, would sail to your land this month? And that you, on receiving my message, took a barge and journeyed all this way in order to receive this boy?"

"Yes, Ahikar, this is so."

"Well, Het-Ka-Sebek, today, your eyes have been satisfied that my words were true. And now tell me, could there be a rarer gift with which your god—may his mercy shine upon you forever—would be more satisfied than this?"

"There is a certain girl within the bounds of the Temple whose body is also without blemish, and moreover, she is a most comely child. A servant of the Temple caught her in his fishing net while she was bathing in a lake. She is a child of the Upper Kingdom. Her parents were filled with joy when they received twenty sacks of barley from the captain of the barge who had wandered about the land in search of a pleasant offering for Sebek."

He lowered his head and fell silent.

"Twenty sacks of barley!" spoke Ahikar softly but also with an air of untold contempt as though he had heard of an evil crime. "Do you really believe, Het-Ka-Sebek, that twenty sacks of barley can suffice to buy an offering for a god as great as yours?"

And he fell silent. The tall Egyptian coughed and looked angrily at the workers and the scribe, for they had overheard their conversation.

Quickly the scribe signaled with his hand for the unloading to proceed and returned to his scroll. The first of the workers arrived with a bale of cloth which they placed down carefully upon the reed mats outstretched before the table and walked back to the ship. Thus the unloading continued.

"Remember, Het-Ka-Sebek, Guardian of the Living Effigy of the Soul of Sebek, the god, it was you who asked me how the Temple could repay me for my troubles. And so I tell you, this boy, a gift of the sea and an immaculate offering, is worth no less than two hundred and fifty rolls of papyrus, and each roll must be thirty ells long. But countless years of exchange between your Temple and the house of my forefathers give me occasion to offer up to your god two score rolls and ten of papyrus, and therefore you will pay me only two hundred rolls for the boy."

47

The priest looked up sharply.

"For one young slave? This is madness, Ahikar!"

"No, Het-Ka-Sebek, Peace Guardian of the Living Effigy of the Soul of Sebek, the god. By demanding this and no other price, I merely wish to show you, even though I am not one of your people, that I, too, am eager to pay homage to your god. I shall speak openly, for it is no intention of mine to offend you with the crafty or devious words typical of those who demand exorbitant prices at first, only to reduce them gradually, all the while plucking at their beards in false despair and then rejoice at home for having fooled their buyers with such eloquent talk. Though my price may sound unreasonable to you, it is smaller than the offering is truly worth. But I shall not venture to demand a greater payment from your mighty god, Sebek. Only from some minor gods, some pagan Nubian divinity of a tiny riverside town, could I have the right to expect more. But let minor merchants trade with minor gods. Therefore, do not treat me as a stall keeper or a pauper at a time when the granaries are running out of supplies, and everyone is forced to sell his own children for a mere twenty sacks of grain."

Het-Ka-Sebek knitted his brow and opened his mouth as though wishing to answer harshly, but he made no sound. Instead, he looked at the boy for a while and, in silent contemplation, started drawing some small figures in the sand. Then he ran his bare foot with golden painted toenails over its surface.

"Two hundred rolls of papyrus is a great deal to ask, Ahikar, but great also is the god I serve. I shall leave now and take him with me..." He pointed to Whitehair with his staff.

"When you have finished unloading your ships and filled them up again with my merchandise, order one of your captains to remain behind for fourteen days. On the fifteenth day, he will see a boat upon the river, and in it, there will be a priest who will give him the papyri. As for the silver from the northern lands, which you mentioned earlier, and for which my Temple gladly exchanges its Nubian ivory, and which we will continue exchanging in the future in a way that is beneficial to us both, we have already struck a bargain. If some unforeseeable event should take place, you will inform the House of God. Or should you die, may one of your sons, the one who will succeed to your fortune, confirm our agreement. And many thanks to you for this offering which you have given my God and Master."

"Truly, your Master is a Great God," Ahikar bowed humbly, "if his favor can be won even by a worthless piece of living dust, which I surely am before his eyes. It, therefore, gladdens me beyond measure that I, a mere foreigner, can serve him too. Farewell to you, Het-Ka-Sebek, Peace Guardian of the Living Effigy of the Soul of Sebek, the god."

"Farewell, Ahikar. May a favorable wind and your experienced oarsmen guide you safely to the port of Gubal, and moreover, when you reach home, may your aging eyes be filled with joy upon seeing your sons and grandsons."

They bowed once more, and then, without even looking at Whitehair, the old merchant returned to his ships.

The priest thrust his staff into the sand and clapped his hands.

Immediately, someone ran up from the group of people standing close by and placed a small chest at the feet of Het-Ka-Sebek. It was made of variegated woods and encrusted with silver and stones. The one who had brought it stepped back and, with half-bent back, watched the priest, who gave him an order with his hand.

At once, he opened the chest and, balancing himself on one knee, took out a golden loincloth and an alabaster vial.

Het-Ka-Sebek took hold of the vial, opened it, and approached Whitehair. To the accompaniment of strange words which he pronounced slowly and nearly soundlessly, the priest poured a few drops of thick, greenish fluid onto his palms. Then with the tips of his fingers, he touched the young Trojan upon the forehead and chest and, lifting the golden loincloth, fastened it around his waist. At last, he retreated a few steps and bowed down solemnly.

Whitehair stood still, unable to grasp what was happening to him. A sudden shiver of fear ran down his spine as he faced the unknown, for he realized now that Ahikar had left him to these people. But to what purpose? If he were treated as an ordinary slave, he would grieve over his pitiful fate, but at least he would know what it meant and what could happen to him.

But as things stood—was he a slave at all? For who would dress a slave in a loincloth worthy of kings, anoint his body, and bow down before him? No land could practice such things, and he was sure that this one, too, could be no different. No people on earth would ever do such a thing. No one worshipped slaves.

Instinctively he looked at the one who had spoken the Trojan tongue. No other person could possibly give him an answer. The priest, who appeared to have read the meaning in his eyes, uttered a few words.

And now, the one who had spoken to Whitehair in the Trojan tongue approached quickly. He fell to his knees and placed his palms on the ground, and remaining where he was, spoke:

"Hail, O Son of Sebek, O one who longs to join his father! Hail, for from the waters thou hast come, and unto them thou shalt return!"

"What are you saying?" asked Whitehair, still full of fear, though he did not know what frightened him. "Why are you kneeling in front of me and treating me like a son of a god or king? You know that my father is a fisherman. What have I done to make you look at me like this? Who do you think I am?"

"Once the son of a fisherman," said the other one rising, his head lowered and eyes cast down in reverence. "Today the hand of god has descended upon you, his eyes have seen your body, and he has anointed you his son. Het-Ka-Sebek, my master, brings news of your father, who longs for your presence and wishes to unite himself with you on the day of his feast!"

The priest uttered a few more words, and the servant

translated:

"The barge of god awaits you. The most venerable Het-Ka-Sebek, Peace Guardian of the Living Effigy of the Soul of Sebek, the god, invites you humbly onto its deck, for a long journey stands ahead of us along the waters of the great river, and your father is anxious to set his eyes upon you."

Whitehair did not answer. He lowered his head, and his lips began to move, but no one could hear his whisper:

"Mother! Giver and taker of life, Great Mother, I beseech you, guide me back to the land where I belong..."

And in a quieter voice, he added:

"Alive."

He looked up.

"If such is the will of this venerable priest," he said quietly, trying to steady his voice and make it sound like the voice of a grown man, "let us move on."

He stepped forward and looked at the tall Egyptian who signaled with his hand. Four dark-haired pipers swayed forward out of the waiting group and, putting their two-tubed instruments to their mouths, played music and moved in dancing strides along the beach.

Het-Ka-Sebek bowed, took the boy by the hand, and together they followed the piping girls. His palm was cold and soft, like the palm of a woman.

Whitehair ignored the ships along the coast and moved on, knowing that each vessel was full of inquisitive eyes, all of them peering in his direction.

They walked along the edge of the warm, damp beach, bathed in the shadow of tall palm trees, licked by the tongues of tiny waves.

He could hear the whisper of many feet. Undoubtedly the priest was being followed by his entire retinue. Only the piercing lament of flutes constantly rose and fell, and nobody spoke a word. Not the slightest wind was blowing. And now Whitehair recalled the morning he had gone fishing when the same kind of dreadful silence prevailed, and he wondered whether he would ever go fishing again.

Presently, they reached the place where the shore formed a small gulf. It was some time before he noticed a beautiful sky-blue ship with a white sail supported by two slightly slanted spars.

And he knew at once, even before the pipers ahead of him had time to stop on either side of the gangplank which had been thrown from the deck to the shore and covered with a purple carpet, that this was their ship.

He walked along with the tall priest, who held him by the hand, and stepped onto the deck. Het-Ka-Sebek led him towards some chairs of carved wood that stood on a platform and, releasing his hand, indicated one of them.

Whitehair sat down.

The priest slumped into the neighboring chair and nodded to the one who had spoken to Whitehair earlier. The man came forward and sat at their feet.

Strange and sharp commands pierced the silence.

The dark-skinned slaves drew the gangplank in and placed it beside the oarsmen. Presently they took hold of long, variegated poles and, on hearing the captain call an order, forced them into the sand. The ship stirred and withdrew from the shore. Whitehair looked at the priest who was sitting on his chair, clasping both its arms firmly. Clearly, he was not accustomed to life upon the waters.

But the ship sailed along smoothly now, and the oars which had been raised up high dipped, driving it forward.

"Could we be making for the open sea?" thought Whitehair, and at once, it flashed through his mind that if, at night, the moon and stars revealed land, he could jump into the water while the priest and the rowers were asleep. But no, it could not be, for the one who sat at his feet had already told him that a long river journey awaited them! And this river flowed through the land of the watery god, to whom he had been offered so that even if he did escape, the people dwelling along its banks would surely capture him and hand him over.

But how could he escape when he hardly knew where he was? His native land must lie to the north, for Ahikar's ship had sailed south for two whole days and nights and then again for another four days and nights with favorable wind and with the help of oars toward the southeast. And then, from Gubal to Egypt, they also sailed south, though also a little to the west. And so his home was to the north. But how far from here was it? Even if he had a ship of his own, it would take at least a week to reach it?

He shook his head, wishing to disperse such foolish thoughts which merely weakened the heart and brought nothing but the taste of bitter tears.

The ship was approaching the wide estuary of a river. And now the priest spoke.

"Rejoice, for on the seventh day, you shall see your father!" And the one at his feet joyfully explained these words. "My master says that you shall be at one with god, your father, on the day of the great feast, when the waters of the river subside and the time of great fishing in the lake begins."

Whitehair opened his mouth, for he wished to ask the name of the river, but just then, two slave girls approached with jugs and mugs containing beverages, and behind them, two more with roasted fowls.

Picking the meat off the fowl, he looked at the banks of the river as they unfolded before his eyes, at the distant city with its tremendous temple, and finally at the flatness of the land. Nowhere, wherever he looked, could he see the slightest eminence. The river flowed along lazily. Its wide current of turbid, greenish waters mingled with the sea of reeds and stretched on forever in the distance, filling the world with nothing but its own murky color.

A piece of canvas was stretched above their heads. The girls returned with fans of large and slightly frayed plumes fixed on long light rods.

One of them, humming softly, stood behind Whitehair and fanned him steadily.

The young Trojan closed his eyes, but still, a great fear gripped his heart.

"What is happening?" thought he. "Why are they paying homage to me? This is so very strange."

He shuddered, for it now occurred to him that they were revering him like some kind of an offering to be sacrificed on the altar of their mysterious god, whom they called his father.

Again his eyes opened and closed. The wind in the large sail began to murmur like the sea. A silent humming filled the air. Whether it was the girl with the fan, or the distant Song of the Quern, he did not know.

"Will they burn me on the altar?" he thought drowsily and was surprised at his indifference. The question dissolved, and everything
began to fade until at last, he could neither see nor hear... and soon he fell asleep.

CHAPTER FOUR
I Live, But He Lives Not

"They call me Lauratas. Or rather, that is what they used to call me in my fatherland," explained the one who, for three days now, had been translating the words of Het-Ka-Sebek.

The ship approached a great city, looming out of the distance, and expanding on both sides of the river. The priest had risen and walked away towards the bow, leaving them alone.

"Are you a slave?"

The one who sat at his feet remained silent and stared at the water. From time to time, the forest of tall reeds parted, and tiny villages or cities with tall temples were revealed.

"Yes, I am a slave. Once I was a seafarer, and my liege was the king of Knossos, ruler of Crete and the islands of the sea. We were shipwrecked on the Libyan coast, a little to the west of the place you landed. Only two of us survived. We were captured by the people of the coast and sold to Egypt. For twenty years now, I have served as a slave in the Temple of the god Sebek which lies by the Great Lake. I do not complain about my fate, for the temple has made me the steersman of its boats. And now I am here with Het-Ka-Sebek, who took me along with him, for he knows that you are from the north and that our tongues must be similar, if not the same."

"But what happened to your companion, the one who was captured with you?"

"He was united with Sebek."

"What does that mean?"

"In time, everything shall be revealed to you."

And again, they fell silent. The great barge sailed on without the slightest sway. A monotonous voice could be heard from the deck below. It was the driver monotonously intoning the tempo for the rowers to follow. The oars rose steadily and descended in tiny splashes. Now that all the reeds had disappeared, a world of white clay huts could be seen littering the stretch of lowland. An immense harbor paved with stone slabs came into view and then a wide alley leaning towards a temple in the distance. And this temple glared in the sun, for its walls seemed to be made of sparkling water.

"Whose temple is this?"

"They call it Per-Bast, which means the house of the goddess Bast, who is a she-cat."

"What? A cat?"

"These people worship different animals in different parts of their land. Their land stretches along both sides of this river and is surrounded by a vast sea of waterless sands. Here they adore Bast with the head of a she-cat, but our Lake is ruled by Sebek, and no cat will ever be worshipped there. However, there are temples which hold other gods sacred, and the whole of Egypt worships the sun and the gods of the Underworld, and these are revered everywhere."

"Who is this Sebek?"

The sitting one lifted his head instinctively to look around, but the priest was still at the bow talking to the captain.

"He is an almighty god..."

Whitehair barely heard his whisper. "They call him Lord of the Seas, for the lake is named Paium, which means 'the sea,' though it is not as big as the sea we know."

"Is this god a fish?" asked Whitehair with seeming composure, as if the answer was unimportant.

Just at this moment, two large rafts were passing them heading upstream, and they were carrying heavy blocks of stone. The current forced them off course a little so that the barge had to move towards one of the banks in order to avoid a collision. And at once, loud shouting arose from both decks.

"He feeds on fish, though he himself is something else. You saw him yesterday and two days ago, for he often likes to sunbathe along the banks of this river."

"And the staff of Het-Ka-Sebek, your master, depicts the head of this creature?"

"You are wise."

Whitehair opened his mouth but hesitated and looked at the river. The rafts had already passed their ship, but many more boats and ships could be seen on the water, for the city extended a great distance along both banks. It was much larger than could have been expected from afar. The priest still remained at the bow, leaning on his staff and gazing into the current.

"And I am to be his Son?"

"Yes."

"But what does this mean?"

"It means that you shall be worshipped as never before, for indeed, even the high priest himself shall never taste homage as great as yours."

"Until I join him?"

"Yes."

"And how will this take place?"

"You shall see."

"Why hide secrets within your heart?"

"I am a slave. I know that those who forget their tongues perish in agony."

"Do not be afraid, Lauratas. I know I am only a boy, but I can understand you well and know how your friend joined Sebek. He was thrown to that monster and devoured, and the same fate awaits me."

"O silence, silence, wretched one..." said Lauratas looking the other way and hardly moving his lips. "Unless you wish my death, please, I beg you, be silent!"

Whitehair also noticed through the corner of his eye that Het-Ka-Sebek was approaching. He was smiling, and he sat down comfortably to the right of the boy. Nodding to Lauratas, he uttered a few words.

"It is with great regret that my master, Het-Ka-Sebek, Guardian of the Living Effigy of the Soul of Sebek, the god, informs you that we are moving somewhat slower than would be desired, for we have only covered a third of the journey. But be not distressed, says he, for the longer you wait, the greater will be the joy of meeting your father." Whitehair did not answer.

On the evening of the ninth day, the thick sycamore wood growing beyond the bend in the river parted and revealed the endless walls of a city-temple.

"My master says that your wanderings are drawing to a close," translated Lauratas. "Rejoice, O Son of God, for shortly you will behold the house of your father!"

The priest continued: "You will be blissful, and every wish of yours shall be fulfilled until the greatest of them all shall meet your eyes— the unity with god."

"Ask your master," said Whitehair, surprised at his boldness, "if I can have one of my wishes now."

Het-Ka-Sebek listened and leaned toward the boy.

"Speak, and every wish of yours shall be granted."

"I would like... I would like you to accompany me here, for there are many things I wish to learn about my father and the house he dwells in. Ask your master, therefore, if he may allow you to be my guide."

The priest answered briefly, pointing out the boy to Lauratas, who came forward, prostrated himself, and embraced the young Trojan, kissing his feet and calling out aloud:

"Master, my life is in your hands!"

"Get up!" Whitehair said quickly. "Your actions bring nothing but shame upon us both. Neither of us is free. Remember, I am a man just like you."

Lauratas heaved himself onto his knees and moved back a little. Next, he rose and bowed down, almost touching the ground.

Het-Ka-Sebek touched Whitehair's shoulder just as the ship emerged from a bend in the river, and now a vast sheet of untroubled water expanded before their eyes.

It was a lake, in the middle of which two enormous pyramids of stone rose up like islands. Their summits were occupied by a pair of immense figures depicting humans sitting upon thrones and looking down from above.

To the right, a tremendous white temple surrounded by rich gardens touched the shore.

The sun had set, and Whitehair stood in silence, watching the distant temple drawing closer.

"Your journey, O son of god, has reached its end!" said Het-Ka-Sebek. "Behold, this is the house of your father!"

In the growing dusk, they approached the stone landing stage, illuminated by the light of torches. Whitehair saw a long wide alley lined on either side by statues of resting lions. There were a great many people upon the landing stage.

In absolute silence, Het-Ka-Sebek took the young Trojan by the hand, and together they proceeded toward the gangplank. But before they reached it, the priest stopped and said a few words in a resounding voice.

Shouting arose, and torches started waving about, filling the stone path of the temple with a wild dance of flaming flashes. The sound of drums and many other instruments which Whitehair had never seen before poured out of the shadows, lively, noisy, and rhythmical, producing a strange kind of music.

They started to descend. The music and shouting died down, and a dead silence fell as they walked on. Whitehair could hear the whisper of his feet as they stroked the smooth stone slabs. Het-Ka-Sebek accompanied him and continually held his hand.

The swarthy, naked people standing on either side of the bronze gates of the temple remained motionless, holding torches in outstretched arms.

Het-Ka-Sebek stopped in front of them, raised his staff, and struck the gates with its handle.

Four loud metallic notes.

Silence.

Noiselessly the huge, shining leaves of the gates started opening inwards. Het-Ka-Sebek and Whitehair stepped in slowly. Inside there was an enormous courtyard surrounded by a forest of formidable columns which reached up and disappeared in the darkness overhead. A solitary old man was standing there holding a torch.

They walked towards him, and just as they were close enough for Whitehair to see the strange symbols embroidered on his long white robe, the old man lifted his torch. They stopped, and Het-Ka-Sebek bowed down humbly.

"Who are you?" asked the old man.

He spoke in a hoarse and quiet voice, but the echo of his words grew louder in the gloom of the invisible vaults and faded again.

"O most venerable father of the house of god!" Het-Ka-Sebek answered in a loud voice. "I am the one whom they call the Peace Guardian of the Living Effigy of the Soul of Sebek, the god, and I have here his son who will join him and rule the world with his father!"

"Greetings to you!" The old man stretched forth his hand and passed the torch to the priest. "Take the Son of Sebek to a place of rest, and at daybreak, let him look upon his father from afar, for the time of unity has not arrived yet!"

"It shall be done, O father of the house of god!"

At dawn of the following day, Lauratas came to him.

"Master! The sun is rising, and the priests wish to show you to your father!"

Whitehair opened his sleepy eyes. He sat up on his bed covered with soft animal skins, the kind of which he had never seen before. He looked at Lauratas, who was holding a silver basin and a variegated linen towel.

He rose, took the basin, splashed some water onto his face, and wiped himself with the towel.

Lauratas clapped his hands. At once, four slaves slipped in with the morning meal, removed the towel and basin, and silently disappeared through the entrance, curtained off by figured material.

"Have you eaten?" Whitehair indicated his own meal of bread and fruit.

But the serving man shook his head and bowed down.

"I am not worthy to partake of food before the son of god. Master, how can I serve you now?"

The young Trojan opened his mouth to tell him not to speak to him in such a way when they were alone, but Lauratas quickly placed his finger on his lips and bowed down once again.

Whitehair sat down and nourished himself, but his eyes constantly wandered about the room with great curiosity. Slowly, his thoughts returned to him and again he realized why he was here. After a while, he rose and looked at the entrance, saying:

"Shall we go out?"

"Yes, master."

They walked along endless tall corridors. Columns surrounded the courtyard through which they passed, and these appeared to be quite different from the ones Whitehair had seen the previous evening. And now they passed a few more empty rooms and then a stone passage leading towards the gardens of the temple.

They were alone now. They had met no one on their way.

Whitehair walked along the path of soft golden sand lying in the shade of palms, sycamores, and clumps of thick, strange shrubs. The glades between the trees were full of sky-blue flowers and striped, deer-like animals with strange twirling horns, clearly accustomed to people, for they continued to graze in their presence.

"This god, where is he?" asked Whitehair. These were the first words he had spoken since they left.

"Master, you will now see him." Lauratas indicated the path

along which they were walking.

"Do not speak to me like that when you and I are alone! We are from the same people, and you are older than me. We are alone now, and no one can hear us. Are you so frightened that you believe their ears can reach us here?"

The Cretan lowered his voice.

"Their eyes and ears are everywhere. And above all, beneath the temple roof, one must keep a cautious tongue, for it is known that there are corridors in the walls from which everything in the chambers can be heard and seen. Even here, it is not safe because if someone happened to stand behind a shrub, someone who knows our tongue, he could easily overhear our words."

"Let me question you..."

"Wait," breathed Lauratas.

They turned right and walked onto a meadow, from which a view of the lake unfolded before their eyes.

The two stone pyramids rising out of its waters and crowned by two giant statues appeared to Whitehair somewhat smaller than on the previous day when he had seen them from the barge. But the lake was undoubtedly vast, for its opposite shore was not visible.

A small temple stood on the edge of the meadow beside the lake. Lauratas guided Whitehair towards it.

Only when they had passed the last of the thickets and left them a long way behind did he speak more freely:

"He will be fed shortly, and you will see all for yourself."

"When shall I be sacrificed?" asked Whitehair quickly.

"Do not question me! Do you want me to perish before you? What will you gain if I tell you?"

Whitehair walked more slowly.

"I am young and inexperienced..." he said. "But no beast, even the most ferocious, I say, can defeat the weakest of all creatures if the Mother of the People does not wish it."

"Each day for twenty years, I have prayed to her, begging to see my native shores again, though I know that even she cannot grant me this..." breathed Lauratas, "because this land is a land of no return."

"But there is no one guarding us here!"

"But what is the point of guarding us?! This beautiful lake, together with its surrounding woods and fields under crop, is a mere island floating on the sea of sands, of endless expanses, where there is neither a drop of water nor a blade of grass. And the only way out of here is along the river. The desert boundaries and river banks are crowded with guards. In this land where all property and all people are known and counted, and where no one changes his place of stay without the knowledge and permission of the officers, you could not remain anywhere for long unnoticed! You would be caught at once, and needless to say, your fair hair and white skin would cause a great stir wherever you went. Many years ago, I thought of this myself, and there were times when I yearned to glimpse my homeland, and this yearning of mine became greater than my fear. Then I was ready to fly, fostering the smallest of hopes, but alas, I still found no way to run. This is why they allow you to walk about freely. You are imprisoned, and yet you hardly know it."

"But when... when shall I be sacrificed?"

"This river feeds the whole of Egypt, and its waters rise high then fall each year, every year. No one knows why, but it has always been so. The waters start to rise in late spring. But a long time must pass before they reach their highest point, stay there, and then begin to subside. When the river is high, the river water rushes into this lake furiously, but it has nowhere to go because it is desert sand all around us here. There is no outlet. So the water stays high, and when the water in the river falls, it begins to subside, too. At present, the water is still rising, but the day when it stops rising and begins to subside is imminent. When this happens, the days of great fishing shall commence, for there is much fish here, and men and crocodiles feed upon them. And on that day, it will be time to unite your mortal body with Sebek."

"How much time is left?"

"If I am to speak the truth, the sun will cross the heavens no more than nine times or maybe ten."

"Do they... slay their offerings first?"

"No! You will approach the pool where Sebek dwells and throw yourself to him. You will feel no fear, for great joy shall descend on your body."

"Are you saying that I will find myself suddenly overjoyed to find my death in the jaws of this god?"

"They will bring you a fluid the color of wine, and it will fill you with the greatest joy at the prospect of imminent unification, and your fear will be gone. And when they lead you there in the ceremonial procession..."—here he pointed towards the small temple which they were approaching—"it will gladden your heart to know that you are the central figure of this ceremony, and you will refuse nothing, and do everything they ask of you to do, and you will show your jubilance."

"Mother..." breathed Whitehair and shuddered, for a sudden shiver chilled his body.

"Pray, be silent!" added Lauratas quickly. "Here is the place where their god dwells, and shortly you will witness his morning feast. But I implore you, show no emotion at the sight, for if they suspect me of revealing your fate, I too shall perish a most torturous death!"

They stopped before the brownstone temple overlooking a large pool, its shimmering surface encircled by a low stone wall. In the middle of the pool, there was a small island covered with shrubs, a white marble plinth towering above them. A god of red stone occupied its throne. His body was human, but his head was that of a crocodile, with jaws half open.

Lauratas fell to his knees and touched the ground with his forehead and outstretched palms.

"Follow my actions!" he whispered, and Whitehair prostrated himself beside him.

"Their eyes are on us..." murmured the Cretan, "and they can see everything from the windows of the temple."

After a while, he lifted himself off his knees and, bowing down to the statue on the islet, whispered:

"Do you see him?" And now he spoke out aloud: "O son of god, behold your father!"

At first, Whitehair thought that his words were directed at the statue and its hideous head. But now, suddenly, he saw him. An enormous beast was resting on the stretch of sand which descended towards the water. It was motionless, and its tail lay hidden amongst the shrubs.

The crocodile moved its head slowly, rose onto its short legs, and settled back onto the sand. A flash of the sun accompanied its movements, for its hocks were wrapped with golden bracelets, and either side of its head was adorned with earrings set with precious stones. Whitehair stared in horror, unable to move.

So this was Sebek, the god, the father, the thing he was meant to join. Nine or ten more days and those monstrous jaws would crush his bones, and its fearsome teeth would be stained by the color of his blood!

The sound of chanting floated across from the small temple, but his thoughts were too deep for him to hear.

"They are coming," whispered Lauratas, retreating and falling to his knees. Whitehair looked round.

Four priests, all dressed in white, were approaching.

And between them, they led a white goat which treaded along calmly, completely indifferent to their chanting. As they approached the stone embankment, they bowed solemnly before Whitehair and stood still.

Presently, Het-Ka-Sebek appeared, approached the others, and also bowed before Whitehair, who, upon seeing him, lowered his head.

Suddenly the four priests lifted the goat and, still chanting, hurled it into the pool. For a while, he could see four slender legs hovering in the air. Then the water splashed. Het-Ka-Sebek stepped towards the stone border and stretched forth his arms, crying out in a brief but resounding voice. The priests fell silent.

The goat had already started swimming towards the edge of the pool, its legs disturbing the crystal clear water as it desperately struggled to climb out. But the vertical wall was made of a smooth stone which gave the goat no support at all.

Whitehair looked at the tiny island.

The heavy body remained lifeless for a while, but presently it stirred and slid into the water.

The crocodile moved along smoothly, taking its time and leaving the water undisturbed. Only its small protruding eyes could be seen above the surface. The beast produced only small, infinitesimal ripples, barely noticeable as they scattered across the pool.

As the creature drew nearer, the goat, which had already guessed its doom, suddenly leaped out of the water in one final throw of despair. But it slipped back into the pool.

Then the water seethed, and the goat disappeared. Whitehair noticed the crocodile violently whipping its tail as it lunged for the bottom with its offering. Then, gradually the surface of the pool changed its color to red.

A shower of sunrays descended onto the turbid water, and now it was impossible to see what was happening in the depths.

The chanting increased in speed and pitch. Suddenly it stopped. Het-Ka-Sebek lowered his arms, turned round, and withdrew with his head lowered. His arms were crossed over his chest. The remaining priests followed in pairs.

Whitehair looked at the islet. The crocodile was climbing onto it backward, dragging something along. Its enormous tail swept the sand, its hind legs and body emerged, and at last, its jaws holding something dreadful: the deformed offal of what had recently been a slender white goat.

Whitehair turned round and walked up to Lauratas, who was still down on his knees.

"Rise!" he breathed. "Now I know how I will join my father, the great god Sebek."

He attempted to smile but found it impossible. A spasm gripped his throat, and he bit his lip because he did not want to burst into tears.

The Cretan rose, and together they crossed the meadows towards the lake.

"So you think I am lost and beyond all hope?"

"Yes, young Trojan. I am sure of it, for you will find no one willing to help you here. And yet the gods do not grant long life to everyone. You will live until the day of your death, which has been marked out for you long before you even saw the light of day."

"Do you mean to tell me that I am to enter those monstrous jaws with my head down, doing nothing to avoid such a fate?"

"What else can you do?"

They stopped beside the shore. Birds were hovering over the lake, and its surface was full of boats sailing in various directions. Whitehair breathed in profoundly and gritted his teeth.

"This land must be very fertile," he said almost calmly, looking towards the horizon. "There is no sand here."

"The sand begins just beyond those palm groves which grow along the banks. When the winter winds arrive, the fields get buried in sand, and the sand must then be removed. This conflict between man and desert has gone on since the beginning of time. Here, nourishment is provided by the lake, and in the rest of Egypt, by the river. Water is the mother of life, for, without it, everyone would soon perish."

"And what lies to the north of here?"

"To the north, the river flows as far as the sea, six or seven days down current. But to the west, there is nothing but sand. Beyond these fields," Lauratas pointed to the right bank of the lake, "lies the City of the Dead, a place where those great lords who have died are buried but first their bowels are removed, and their bodies are soaked for three score days and ten in various fluids which preserve them. Then, once they are placed in their tombs, they remain unchanged forever. You see, the souls of those who have lived in honesty return each day to the world of the living, but at night they must descend to the land of the dead, where the god Osiris rules. The richer a man is, the more beautiful and safer his tomb will be, for the chamber containing his mortal remains will be hidden in a rock or under a building of stone so that his body will remain untouched. You see, here, in this land, there is life after death only as long as their bodies remain preserved."

"And what will happen to me once I am devoured by this creature? Will not I, the offering of their god, be endowed with life after death?"

"When Sebek devours his offering, the offering unites with him."

"Ah. You have given me courage," smiled Whitehair sadly.

They walked back to the small temple and the pool.

"It will surprise you, Lauratas, but I would like to see Sebek on his islet again."

"No!" the Cretan shook his head. "It does not surprise me, for now, you find yourself in the shadow of death, and I shall mourn you according to our custom. I shall kindle you a small fire, far from the eyes of mortals, and implore the gods to accept you into the Meadows of Asphodel."

They were passing the smaller temple, and Whitehair noticed it contained mysterious images and carved symbols.

"Do you know the meaning of these signs?" asked Whitehair.

"Yes, for I have learned a few things about their writing, though none of them know this," whispered Lauratas. "Here, on the front of the temple, are written the words of the scroll which is placed on the chest of one who has died so that he may pass unhindered into the blissful land of Osiris. Do you wish to know what these words are?"

"Yes," Whitehair stopped.

"It says: 'I am the one who reigns in the midst of fear. I am the god Sebek. I pounce upon my prey with a blood-thirsty ferocity. I am the god, the one before whom everyone bows and prostrates himself in Sekhem.'"

"Is this city called Sekhem?"

"Yes."

They approached the pool.

To his great surprise, Whitehair noticed a little girl standing beside the water with an old priest. Her skin was dark. She was playing with a leather ball, throwing it up toward the sky, and she was laughing and calling to the priest. But the priest took hold of her hand and led her away from the stone border of the pool.

"She... is your sister," muttered Lauratas. "On the feast day, you two shall be sacrificed together."

Whitehair stopped suddenly and watched the retreating child, her tiny legs toddling along beside the white robe of the priest. She was so much younger than he was, and yet his sister in death.

He stopped beside the stone border and looked into the pool.

"Is the god also unable to climb out and free himself?"

"That is correct. He entered this pool as a baby crocodile after the death of his predecessor and thus became the eternal prisoner of the islet. But he does not hanker for anything, for as you see, he is well nourished. His brothers on the lake and on the great river are less spoiled and much more nimble. He has no need to fight for survival or nourishment, and this has made him lazy."

Whitehair stood still and watched the resting creature, bathing in the heat of the sun. His feast was finished. There was nothing left. Unlike wolves and panthers of the Troad, this beast devoured all: flesh, bones, head, and horn.

The young Trojan shuddered again.

In silence, they moved towards the great temple whose lofty roofs and towering columns could be seen above the tree tops.

Whitehair looked up. Many beautiful horses with purpled manes and tails were grazing in the meadow.

Lauratas answered before Whitehair could ask:

"No, they do not ride horses. Only the desert guards do—in order to defend the border against the savage people of the wilderness who sometimes break in and ravage villages that lie close to the sea of sand. But the temple possesses horses of its own, and if you wish to ride tomorrow, your wish will be granted you, for Het-Ka-Sebek has said that whatever you desire, you will receive."

Whitehair nodded.

"Let them provide us with horses on the morrow. We shall go riding or take a bow and spear and hunt some wildfowl that hovers over the lake. If I am to perish in this place, let these last days of mine be filled with a little joy. I refuse to waste time on contemplating death."

Lauratas bowed his head.

"Your words are fitting, for you speak like a grown man and not like the mere boy which you really are. For he who is a coward dies a thousand deaths, and he who is not, dies but once. I shall see that everything will happen according to your will."

And so, on the next day, when Whitehair woke up, he saw two beautiful saddle horses waiting in front of the temple.

They mounted the beasts and rode along the banks of the lake, and when all the buildings had disappeared, they started hunting.

Later they nourished themselves from the bag that Lauratas had brought with him. Since daybreak, they had not spoken of Sebek nor of his islet in the middle of the pool, but Whitehair could think of nothing else. How could he die like an animal led to the slaughter: without struggle, without defiance, as if death at the jaws of that most foul monster was in itself a great joy? But was not Lauratas right? Was there anything he could do?

Slowly they turned towards the city. In a sudden and desperate blast of anger, Whitehair lifted his bow and released an arrow that zipped through the air. A large heron, rising above the reeds, screeched dreadfully and tumbled into the water.

"You have not missed once yet," said Lauratas, who had

jumped off his horse and walked up to him, leading his beast by its bridle. The young Trojan slipped his bow between the leather straps securing his quiver to the side of his horse.

"When I was much younger, I often hunted rabbits," he said, and his thoughts wandered to the hills of the distant coast where he had been born. "My mother would roast them, for we were a poor family, and everything we wished to eat, we had to catch first!"

And he looked into the sea of reeds into which the heron had fallen.

"Let us return now. We have hunted well. People in Troy would say that that was a good omen!"

Lauratas mounted his horse, and slowly, they trotted along the meadow, stretching beside the boggy banks.

"I shall be sad when you depart," said the Cretan unexpectedly. "You are still a boy, but maybe your nearing death has added to your maturity? Or perhaps you have always been wise beyond your age? I do not know. But I treasure the fact that I can speak to you as an equal. And moreover, it is such a delight to speak in the language of our fathers."

Whitehair remained silent. He reached down, snapped the tip of a reed, took out his dagger, and started whittling the reed away, using his knees to control his horse.

What was he to say? Was he to tell him of how he had wept during the night and how he had bitten his lips in order to prevent himself from calling out the name of Great Mother?

He lowered his head.

"Look, the lake is still rising," said Lauratas suddenly. "Maybe this year it will take longer."

"And this will mean that I shall live for a day, or maybe even two days longer, after which the god will slip down from his isle and meet me in the water all the same? Is this what you meant to say?"

But the Cretan did not answer and spurred his horse on.

To their right and beyond the lake wrinkled by a slight breeze, they could see the gardens and the two temples and to their left, a palm grove, and beyond the grove, a chain of rugged mountains completely devoid of vegetation. And beyond those mountains, as Lauratas had already told him, there were crags, ravines, and valleys, where the City of the Dead had been hewn in the rock.

And even further, a vastness of rolling sands stood out clearly against the cloudless blue sky, a sky which was darker than in his native land.

They rode on in silence. In the distance, they could see the peasants working in the fields, picking grapes that grew on small bushes held up by little sticks.

Whitehair turned towards the pool, for they were approaching the gardens of the temple.

The little girl and the old priest were already there.

His sister was playing in the meadow. Whitehair jumped off his horse and let it go out and graze on the grass. Lauratas did the same.

Whitehair walked up to the girl and stretched forth his hands. Though their tongues were different, she was closer to him than any other child. She was his sister.

She understood his gesture and threw the ball in his direction. He caught it and threw it back. The little girl clapped her hands and reached for the ball, but it rolled in between her legs, and she turned round and ran after it right up to the border of the pool. Having grasped it and lifted it above her head, she prepared to make a sweeping motion, but the ball slipped out of her hands and disappeared in the water, and now the little girl lost her balance, gripped the stone border, and screamed.

Whitehair watched as she fell. Everything happened so quickly, but to him, it seemed to last an age.

With a splash, she disappeared.

But he was running before she even touched the water. He did not think of what he was doing, nor did he hear the shouts of Lauratas and the old priest who were standing still, filled with unspeakable terror.

As he reached the edge of the pool, he jumped high into the air just as the crocodile slipped into the water.

The little girl had already emerged and was desperately scratching at the smooth surface of the wall with her tiny hands, searching for some place to gain a grip. But the wall was very smooth, like the surface of burnished metal.

At once, Whitehair tore out his dagger. With eyes wide open, he searched for the enemy beneath the surface. But the creature seemed to be confused by having received two offerings at once, for it stopped a while, looked at the struggling body of the little girl, and then moved in her direction.

But Whitehair had already reached the crocodile.

Everything happened so quickly that he would never be able to recall the order of things. He did not strike the formidable armor of scales covering the god's side, nor did he smite the monster upon its spine. Instead, he embraced it, tucked his head beneath its jaws and paws, and delivered a number of quick, deep blows to its white belly, lashing out blindly and curling up so as to avoid the mighty limbs of the creature, which could easily wrench him away and draw him towards its furious, ravenous jaws.

The monster raged in the water, violently tossing its tail. Whitehair could feel his strength sagging, and he himself was almost out of breath, but then a sudden and dreadful surge of hate for this beast released itself and transformed him into a ferocious animal. He could feel the flesh ripping and surrendering to his dagger. He tore away and stabbed and stabbed and tore away, on and on, until suddenly, the horrific dance came to an abrupt end.

The crocodile was motionless.

Whitehair plunged to the bottom, then thrust himself up towards the surface. Having emerged, he gasped for air and waited for those monstrous jaws to catch his legs and...

And then he saw a pair of outstretched paws and a white belly covered with blood. The beast was floating upon its back.

It was dead.

Just then, he heard the little girl. She was screaming. He swam up to her and lifted her towards the edge of the pool, which she immediately took hold of with both hands and, skillfully pulling herself up, disappeared.

Next, he put his dagger away and, tensing his muscles, jumped with outstretched hands, but he only just managed to catch hold of the edge of the border for a moment. He thought he would slip back, but he held on with determination and pulled himself up, falling face down onto the stone slabs.

The little girl was gone.

Lauratas was kneeling down, his hands covering his face. The old priest stood riveted in place, like a stone image, his mouth wide open, looking upon the young Trojan in great awe as though he had seen Sebek himself emerging out of the pool.

Panting heavily, Whitehair approached the Cretan and pulled his hands away from his face.

"I have slain him," he said, breathing heavily.

Lauratas started.

"You are alive!"

The young Trojan indicated the pool.

"We must fly, Lauratas, for to perish in flight and battle is far better than to accept death under torture. Come! I am going to escape anyway, and if you do not join me, they will kill you. Come, make haste. We must fly!"

Meanwhile, the priest had recovered and, with a dreadful shriek, rushed forward. Lauratas rose. He pushed away the old man, who fell onto the stones, shouting.

They now ran towards the horses grazing nearby.

As they galloped away towards the thickets near the lake, Whitehair looked round. He could see many white figures pouring out of the temple. They were all running towards the pool.

CHAPTER FIVE
I Wish Them Delivered Alive

Het-Ka-Sebek, Peace Guardian of the Living Effigy of the Soul of Sebek, the god, stood motionless before the opened gates of the temple. His head and chest were exposed to the merciless rays of the sun, but he appeared to be in no pain. Lifting his hand to shade his eyes, he peered to his left, scrutinizing the strip of land beside the lake and the palm grove. His face was calm and without expression.

Deep in the courtyard, a group of priests stood in the shadow of the great gate. None of them dared to approach. They were all waiting, just as he was, motionless, holding their breaths.

Suddenly Het-Ka-Sebek stirred. A tiny, dark spot appeared between the grove and the lake, and with each second, it grew larger. The tall priest lowered his hand and observed the lake. At last, he could see the one he had been waiting for.

A sudden clatter of hooves echoed on the stony ground. The rider pulled the reins so hard that his horse reared, but he had already dismounted. He fell upon his knees.

"Seek them out and bring them before me. Alive," said Het-Ka-Sebek quietly. "Why have you, chief of the desert guards, come so late?"

The one upon his knees lifted his head.

"We wasted no time, master. But I was with my warriors on the fringe of the wilderness, as the scribe had commanded. Some of the peasants had seen a huge lion there and said it was devouring their cattle in the pastures. We hunted it down at sunrise among the rocks, deep in the desert, and slew its mate and two cubs. As soon as your messenger reached us, master, which was on our way back to the city, I galloped ahead alone, ordering my warriors to make for the stables, for their horses were greatly tired, and we needed them to be fresh and swift. They will be here shortly, and I shall have a new horse, for this one is too weak to chase after anyone today."

"They have had a good head start," the priest shook his head. "The sun has wandered this far already..." and he indicated the upper corner of the temple, "from here to where it stands now, and they have been free to run all this time."

"Even if the sun were to cross the heavens twice, master, still I would bring them to you alive, as you have ordered. For if the sands of the wilderness or a wild beast fail to claim them, we shall certainly seize them in no time at all."

"Rise!" spoke Het-Ka-Sebek. "The priests who saw their flight say that they rode west and are sure to make for the banks of the lake leading north so as to avoid the villages. The guards on the river have been informed. But if they go that way, their horses will have no chance of crossing the swamp. Almost certainly, they have chosen the opposite direction and will be heading for the sea. One of them has some knowledge of the region around the city and the lake."

"They will not attempt to cross the desert on horseback, master. And too little time has passed for them to outdistance us."

"One of them, almost a child, handles his bow and dagger with amazing dexterity. He is whitehaired, and his skin is like the skin of the people of the north. When you see him, you will recognize him at once. And the other one, he too is not an Egyptian and comes from the People of the Sea."

"I understand, master..." said the chief of the desert guards. They were called Nu-u and were descendants of a nomadic tribe settled in the borderland. He looked around.

A rumble of hooves sounded from afar. But first, a pack of hounds came rushing through the trees, well over two dozen. Their coats were almost white, and they were long-legged with narrow snouts and floppy ears. Presently the riders appeared behind them.

The hounds dashed towards their master, who stood before Het-Ka-Sebek, but a brief piercing whistle stopped them short so that they turned away, whining quietly.

"Make haste," said the priest calmly. "And when you seize them, remember that the mercy of the temple is at times almost as great as the mercy of the god himself. Not one hair is to fall from their heads, even if it should cost you your life. They are to be brought into my presence alive and well."

The warrior prostrated himself and rose. Without a word, he ran up to the others, and one of them came forward, leading a horse. The chief mounted it from a run and uttered a quiet order. Immediately the entire party turned back, galloped away to the right of the lake, and disappeared. The thundering of hooves died down.

Het-Ka-Sebek remained where he was. The flash of a distant spear met his eyes. He knitted his eyebrows and shook his head.

A thousand years had passed since the god had chosen this pool by the temple on the lake, and in all that time, nothing so terrible had happened. And now a boy, a mere child, did this. But was he indeed a boy, or was he some dreadful creature, the envoy of strange and evil powers?

Could evil powers have purposefully placed him before the eyes of Ahikar and commanded the merchant to take the youngster to Egypt? And moreover, could he, Het-Ka-Sebek, have been influenced by them to purchase the slave? If this was the case, was it not a dreadful omen for the temple?

Someone was approaching, and his naked feet could be heard whispering over the surface of the smooth stones. The priest looked up and at once bent forth in a solemn bow.

The old man who had come from the great temple stopped now and raised his hand in greeting.

"News of a most foul nature has come to my ears," his voice was dry and broken. "How did this happen? Why was there no one to protect the effigy of god from that murderous hand?"

"The boy jumped into the pool, O Father of the Temple, and

there he slew our god by tearing at his flesh."

"Was he not thrown into the water?"

"No. Hu-Tepa, who was in charge of the little girl, tells me that the girl fell into the pool by accident and that the boy jumped in after her to save her."

"And so there was no way in which you or any of the other venerable priests could have foreseen the event? And those guilty of carelessness shall suffer no retribution, for this was the will of god?" whispered the high priest. "For this was the will of god..." he repeated inaudibly and walked along the banks of the lake towards the pool. Het-Ka-Sebek followed in silence. And when they reached the stone border, they looked down into the water and upon a tiny crocodile, almost emerald in color, which swam about quickly back and forth. They bowed down humbly and stretched forth their arms.

"Immortal is our Sebek," said the high priest in a louder voice and looked at Het-Ka-Sebek. "Has this young god of ours arrived from the lake?"

"He is the son of the previous god and was born two months ago. The Pool of Kings was his home, where he dwelled with his mother. I ordered him to be brought here without delay."

"You have done the right thing..." The high priest observed the tiny, restless creature, which looked nothing like the powerful monster it would become with the passage of time. "He is too small still to receive a live human offering. The little girl must return to her parents, and they will receive precious gifts, for there was a time when the eyes of god regarded her with favor."

"It shall be done, O Father of the Temple."

"The feast-day of god is near..." The high priest nodded sadly. "What shall we give him? Even an infant is too large for him to devour. And apart from the little girl, which has already entered the holy pool and left it alive and therefore cannot be offered to Sebek again, even if our young god could rip her apart and become united with her, there is no one in the temple who comes from the waters and whose body is clean."

"I have been thinking, O Father of the Temple, and now I believe that the wrath of god shall not descend upon us or upon this consecrated city, for Sebek shall receive his rightful offering."

"I am listening, Het-Ka-Sebek. Speak your mind."

"The desert guards will catch the fugitives alive, for I have commanded them to do so, caring nothing for the trouble it may cost. And when they are brought before me, I shall send for a man who will nourish our god with their bodies by cutting them into tiny pieces. But they will not die at once, for he is skilled in the art of keeping the condemned alive and conscious, even if they have already been quartered."

The old man thought for a while.

"Your words are wise," he said at last. "He must return to god, even though he too entered and left the pool untouched. God has suffered greatly because of him and now will decide how to treat his offering. He cannot die an ordinary death, one intended for mortals. Let him join his father, who will devour him if he wishes. And the other one, his companion, let him perish in similar agonies, but his flesh must be thrown to the fish, for he was a mere slave of the temple and cannot serve as an offering when the great feast day comes."

"It shall be as you have said, O Father of the Temple!"

And slowly, they walked towards the great temple. A slight wind arose and whispered in the palms and sycamores, and this was followed by another breath of air, this time stronger. The high priest stopped and looked at the horizon beyond the lake.

"Do you see, Het-Ka-Sebek?"

"Yes, O Father of the Temple."

Much of the sky was still slate-blue, but to the west, it had turned dark brown.

Yet another, more violent gust of wind wrenched the robes of Het-Ka-Sebek so that now they walked faster and approached the great temple whose roof towered above the trees.

CHAPTER SIX
The Open Sarcophagus of Nerau-Ta

They galloped through the trees and along the banks of the lake for a long time, leaning forward in their saddles and not looking back.

At last, Whitehair turned around. He could still see the roofs of the temple overlooking the trees, but they were a very long way behind them.

Without slowing down, he shouted to Lauratas:

"No one is pursuing us! Which way now?"

As the Cretan turned round, Whitehair saw that his face was overcome with fear.

"What have you done, wretched one? You have slain us both! They will surely seek us out, and then you will regard your previous fate as an unsurpassable joy! We are doomed!"

Whitehair spurred his horse on with his knees and caught up with Lauratas so that they rode side by side now. The young Trojan leaned forward and shouted above the rumble of the hooves beating against the stony banks of the lake:

"Why did you not seize my hand and stop me? You could have done it easily."

Lauratas bent forward, and for a while, they pressed on side by side in silence.

"I could not!" he shouted, suddenly looking the other way. "I hate them all! How could I not? And now I shall perish for this!"

Whitehair looked back again. For some time, he scrutinized the long stretch of shore running as far as the distant trees on the outskirts of the temple gardens. He still could not see anyone coming.

"Why are they not pursuing us?"

"The pursuit will set out shortly!"

They galloped into a broad forest of reeds and pursued a lakeside path. To their left lay the lake, to their right, the fields, and far ahead, a thin line of rugged mountains, beyond which stretched a vast sea of sand.

"Stop!" shouted Whitehair and reined back his horse, causing it to dig into the ground.

Lauratas continued to gallop in a stooping position but stopped presently and turned back. They waited, hidden from mortal eyes, completely surrounded by tufts of reeds.

"We are lost," whispered the Cretan, breathing heavily. "We are lost, and nothing can save us."

Whitehair shrugged his shoulders.

"We have got bows and quivers full of arrows. And I have a dagger. And if the pursuit comes near, we will defend ourselves. And afterward, let Our Great Lady of the World seal our fates!"

He sat up straight on his horse and paid homage to the goddess by placing his fist to his forehead. Lauratas did the same.

"I would like to have your youth and hope," he said. "Yet, I know them too well. The desert guards watch over the entire region. They are people who serve Egypt, though they are not themselves Egyptian, for they belong to the savage tribes of the wilderness, which once settled on the fringes of the desert. To them, the sands are as familiar as your native home is to you. Their horses are as good as ours and accustomed to long gallops over the desert. And they have hounds!"

"Hounds?"

"Yes, many of them. They are used for tracking down escaped slaves and hunting down wild animals. When they scent our trail, they will chase after us and catch us or drop from exhaustion themselves. And remember the priests. Already they must have alerted the guards around the lake and along the river.

"And we cannot risk crossing over the water because both shores will be full of vigilant eyes throughout the day and night, and the swamps are impenetrable on both banks. But what would it benefit us, even if we managed to cross to the main artery of the Nile? News of us will travel along the water, and guards would seize us in the first village we come to. Anyone who sees you in this land will remember you forever. And even I am obvious to spot, though my skin is a lot darker than yours. Anyway, they will find us shortly. The priests have surely sent for the desert guards, and they will be coming after us before long."

"But for the moment, we are still free!" said Whitehair stubbornly. "Free and in possession of weapons, and the guards and their hounds are still far behind. Our fatherland is to the north beyond the sea. Therefore we must reach the coast. There is no other hope."

"But the river offers no escape. And to reach the sea through the desert on horse or foot would mean a journey of fourteen days, maybe even twenty. I have never heard of anyone attempting such a thing, even though predatory tribes do dwell in the desert somehow. But to go into the desert will mean to fall into their hands, and if we do, they will sell us back to Egypt. I am sure you are well aware what price the temple of Sebek is willing to pay for you!"

"Yes. I think I can guess. But unless you are willing to die today, Lauratas, we have to keep running. I know our chances are small, and our lives are not worth much, but as long as we are free, there is hope. What hope? Nobody knows. But you know these people, and you know this land. How can we lose our pursuers?"

"Lose them? Impossible!" the Cretan shook his head. "There are things you do not know, such as that others have tried to escape. They had planned their escape months in advance, prepared stores of food and water, and yet, they too were caught. But if we are to run, then let it be to the west, to where the mountains meet the lake at its north end. The peasants in the fields will see us and report our movement. But then, instead of going west, we shall head east for the river, which is a journey of a few days, and the mountains will shelter us from prying eyes. Yet, even that may not work. We cannot deceive their hounds."

Whitehair turned back and directed his horse toward the edge of the reeds. He looked about. The road leading from the temple was still empty, and there was no sign of pursuit. The fields were also empty, and only occasionally, a distant figure of a man or a burdened donkey could be seen passing far away.

"We shall do as you say," said Whitehair.

And at once, they galloped towards the remote line of rocky mountains, which stood out distinctly in the sunlight, descending steeply and melting into the grey and expansive waters of the lake. For a long time, they rode on in silence. Gradually the mountains grew larger, and the boundaries of the plowed fields loomed into view.

"Look! There is a man ahead of us!" shouted Lauratas. "Shall we slay him, lest he report seeing us?"

"No. There is no use killing him, for others can see us from afar. Ask him instead about the road to the west. Let them think our destination lies that way."

They approached the half-naked peasant. He stood beside the road with two goatskin water bags in his hands.

"Tell me, peasant, how far is it to the village of Qua-lum?" asked Lauratas, reining in his horse.

"You will be there by sunset, master, or earlier if your horses are fresh," he answered and prostrated himself at the sight of the golden loincloth which Whitehair was wearing. "Blessings unto you, O son of God!"

"Do these bags of his carry water?" asked Whitehair quickly.

"Yes."

"Let him fill them up and give them to us and let us press on without delay. Tell him that the temple will reward him later."

The Cretan spoke to the peasant in a commanding voice, and at once, the peasant ran towards the lake and brought them water.

"Shall we water our horses now?" Whitehair almost whispered, even though the peasant was too far to hear and could not understand their tongue.

"No!" Lauratas looked around instinctively. "We have wasted enough time already. When we reach the mountains, we shall water them. They will have to be fed, also. Otherwise, they will drop before nightfall."

They took the water bags from the peasant and rode on. The mountains were much closer now. They could now see gigantic boulders jutting out of the mountainsides. The road behind them was still empty, and the temple had disappeared from view.

Lauratas slowed down and, touching the neck of his horse, all glistening with perspiration, signaled to Whitehair to rein up.

"Our horses must rest now, otherwise they will not serve us much longer. Look, we have reached the mountains."

He turned towards the water, jumped off his horse, and led it towards the bank.

In silence, they watched their mounts drink.

"Yonder, this road runs beside the lake and along the foot of the mountains, and there we shall turn, but first, we must pass the slope. Then a pathless tract of rocks will lead us east. But after we pass the City of the Dead, we shall encounter nothing but sheer desert until we reach the river. For five whole days! But if they catch up with us, we will perish earlier, and our suffering will be over. To perish in the desert without water is a far kinder death than what we will suffer if they catch us. Even though we are all born the same way, gods end our lives as they wish. If the desert guards appear and there is no further hope of escape, will you kill me? I doubt I will have the courage to do it myself."

"Yes, Lauratas, I will kill you, I promise," said Whitehair calmly, and then I shall kill myself. Our fates are marked out for us already, long before we are born. Therefore, if to die in this desert is our destiny, then we are doomed. But if the gods have sentenced us to die elsewhere, we shall live on, and even a hundred guards with their hounds will do us no harm. Now, to horse!"

They drew their horses away from the water and mounted them. The plowlands dropped behind. And now a scenery of dry and rocky mountainsides covered with tufts of sharp grass unfolded before their eyes.

"We must feed the horses!" shouted Lauratas, looking back at his companion. "And the pursuit is surely on its way! Should we feed them beyond the mountains, where the slopes may have some grass?"

"How much longer can they gallop?"

"Till nightfall!"

"Then we will not feed them! If there is no grass further on, the horses will drop anyway, so not much point feeding them now."

Lauratas waved his arm in despair as if he wanted to say that whether or not the horses were nourished, their fate was sealed all the same.

After they passed the mountainside facing the water, the road bent round gently, shadowing the distant line of palm groves and the city of Sekhem, which lay hidden amongst them. Lauratas stopped his horse.

"We must leave the road and head west, where the mountains will shelter us. And if after sunset they have still not caught us, then we shall think of what to do next."

They entered a narrow valley and it was very stony, and its steep reddish sides were covered with furrows. The ground was clayish so that suddenly the clatter of hooves fell silent.

Lauratas drew in his reins, thus allowing the young Trojan to catch up with him.

"Not far from here, a network of ravines and valleys begins. That is where the dead are buried. Once we are there, it will be difficult to spot us from a distance. If not for the hounds…"

"And later?"

"Later… we shall perish," Lauratas tried to smile. "Nothing can save us. Are you not aware that by hiding in the mountains, we are turning back towards the city in a wide arc?"

"I know, Lauratas. But think of this: maybe our pursuers will never even suspect that, after slaying their god, we chose to meander instead of heading straight into the desert."

"I do not know what the priests will think, but I do know that when the desert guards and their hounds start pursuing us, they will not use the mind of Het-Ka-Sebek. And with the knowledge I have of this land, I know they will catch us by nightfall."

Whitehair did not answer. Instead, he touched his bow, which was slung over his shoulder, and checked whether there was an arrow jutting out of his quiver. The horses started their climb along a gradual slope towards the ridge of the mountain. Without a word, Lauratas pointed. To their left, there was another ravine. One of the rocks which made up its slope was smoothed by the work of human hands and covered with images cut in stone.

"From here, the City of the Dead extends. But we cannot go near it, as there may be people burying their dead there or hewing a new tomb in the rock. As soon as we reach the top of the mountain, we will see the rolling sands of the wilderness, which we must approach by passing around this place. After some time, we shall return to the mountains and keep moving until the sands of the desert stretch before our eyes. And from there on, the gods alone can help us, for the sun will glare down mercilessly, and neither man, beast, nor grass shall cross our path for five full days until we reach the river."

They had almost ascended the mountain when suddenly they felt a gust of wind.

"What was this?" breathed Lauratas and urged his horse on. And now they stood at the top of the ridge, contemplating the vast sea of sands unfolding before their eyes. A stronger gust of wind swept past, producing a small cloud of whirling dust.

"Look!" cried the Cretan. "We are doomed! The great wind draws near!"

Whitehair could hardly believe his eyes. The distant north-westerly heavens had changed their color, and the desert had sprung to life in a billowing haze. A colossal wall of red dust was approaching them. It was a long way off, but the wind started up again, and the sands began to swell.

"Run!" yelled the Cretan. "Back amongst the rocks!" But just then, a tremendous gust of wind hit their eyes. The horses reared, neighing dreadfully. Whitehair dismounted and tried to lead his horse by the bridle, but it tore loose and galloped away with its head down.

The cloud of sand lashed across his face. Half blinded, he noticed Lauratas shooting up into the air and falling onto the ground. He ran up and tumbled down beside him.

The Cretan opened his mouth and shouted something, but his voice was drowned in the noise of the gale.

Darkness fell quickly, but they could still feel the wind whirring the sand across their faces. Whitehair summoned up his strength and shook Lauratas, who rose and followed him down the slope, using his arm to cover his face.

They appeared to be flying down, for the storm was raging behind them, pushing them on. The ravine was narrow, and though the sandstorm was increasing all the time, they managed to slip in between the rocks, cling to boulders, and look about desperately for a hollow in which to shelter.

Another blow, and suddenly Whitehair realized that what he had thought was a dreadful gale was only just its beginning.

The gloom thickened, and the clouds of sand lashed the ravine bottom. He was tossed to the ground. He staggered to his feet but tumbled again. And now he lost sight of Lauratas who was battling on in front of him. His eyes were full of sand, and he was almost blind.

He fell again, struggled up, and gropingly staggered on.

Suddenly someone grasped his shoulder in the darkness and pulled him violently.

The gale had gone. But the hand was still there, and it continued to pull him until he entered complete darkness.

"Be thankful to the gods that I noticed you beside me!" called a hoarse voice. It was Lauratas speaking.

He let go, and Whitehair fell back against a stone wall hidden in the darkness.

"Where are we?" he tried to whisper and started coughing violently. His mouth and throat were full of sand.

"I do not know. This must be the corridor of an unfinished tomb."

Whitehair wiped his eyes and looked at the entrance. It was somewhat higher than where they stood, and the corridor sloped noticeably down as it ran deeper into the rock. A monotonous, dull roar persisted outside, like a furious sea gushing through the ravine. At times puffs of hot air, full of sand, blew into the corridor, causing them to choke. In silence, they joined hands and retreated down the corridor, which dropped rather abruptly and, in one place, turned to the right. They stopped. And now the roar of the gale died away. Now, only a distant murmur accompanied by an acute and muffled whistle reached their ears.

A fit of violent cough overcame Lauratas.

"Great gods..." he whispered, gasping. "O, great gods!"

Do you know what would have happened to us had we been stranded up there?"

But his companion remained silent. He was listening to the howl of the wind. At last, he spoke:

"If a storm like this descends on a mortal in the wilderness, will he live for long?"

"No. For if he falls to the ground, the sweeping sands will bury him. And if he crawls, the storm and desert will choke him in no time. After many years another storm will scatter the mountain of sand which has grown over his body, and a bundle of dry bones will reveal itself beneath the sky. I have seen this on many occasions, not only in the desert but also on the outskirts of cities. Anyone blinded by sand and cast into the depths of the night by day can perish on his very doorstep, and no one will come to aid him because he will be lost to all eyes and ears."

"But you came to aid me..."

"Such was the will of the gods. With the rest of my strength, I covered my face whilst clinging to rocks, and suddenly I stumbled into this corridor. I am a little familiar with this area, and I realized that this had to be the corridor of a tomb or a deep grotto that could give us shelter. Then I turned round and looked into the darkness, and you were right behind."

"Could it be that the gods favor us?" wondered Whitehair. "You said that by sundown, we would be seized by our pursuers. But that is now unlikely to happen. Not tonight."

"Neither man, nor beast, nor indeed any creature can defy the great wind. As long as it rages, we are safe in here."

"And will it also cover up our tracks?"

"Undoubtedly. The hounds will find it difficult to track us down... But remember, we have no water and no horses because they will now be lost in the storm. And what use are these bows of ours without the arrows and quivers with which they galloped away?"

"I have my dagger still," Whitehair hesitated.

"And I have a tinderbox and a blade for striking sparks," said Lauratas. "When the time comes, we can kindle a fire if we can find anything that will burn."

"And to what purpose?"

"Well, in the flicker of the flame, you will get hold of your dagger and kill me, and then you will kill yourself. Are you thirsty?"

"Yes," answered Whitehair quietly. "My throat is burning and full of dust. But we have no water, so why even think of this? Leave your thoughts of death alone, Lauratas, and seek it not, or you may find it. This morning, you were still a slave, and I an intended offering for Sebek. But now you are free for the first time in years, and Sebek became an offering instead of me. Therefore, let us have some hope and await our future."

"You have more courage than I do. I have been a slave too long."

"No, Lauratas. I am only a youth, and I fear death and our pursuers more than you do. But I am determined to live and I know that if I resign myself, all will be lost, but if I go on, there is a chance I may live."

"Perhaps, yes, though I do not know what chance of escape we can possibly have. But you are right. Where there is a spark of hope, it is easy to think that the gods will allow it to glow into a great fire. And therefore, come, let us explore this place and see where the gods have led us to."

And taking hold of his hand, Lauratas lumbered along the dark corridor, running his left hand along the rough cold rock. After a while, he stopped.

"Ho. Ho!" he called out. A distant echo answered him. "We shall go no further in the dark. Some tombs are full of traps laid down against tomb robbers. First, let me light my touchwood if I can find it."

Whitehair heard the sound of two objects striking, then saw a flash of a tiny spark followed by another and then a small flickering in the dark. He strained his eyes, and instinctively placing his hand on his breast, he bared his dagger.

"Look, there is someone standing there!" he whispered.

Lauratas lifted his burning touchwood.

"Ah, a statue," he said calmly. "They serve many purposes. They can be a likeness of the dead person buried here, or they can be guarding food and drink stored here for him. But where are we? It is strange for a tomb to be left unsealed."

He stepped forward, and, raising his dim light, stooped to the ground.

"An oil lamp!" he shouted and touched the wick with his torch. A large flame burst forth, then died down, then a steady flame flared up, producing a soft, warm, yellow light.

"Now I understand! This is the tomb of a mortal who has not been buried yet. Or else, one who has just been buried and whose tomb was about to be sealed but the workers in charge of the job ran away from the storm."

Whitehair looked about in silence. They were standing in a small chamber hewn out of rock. Its walls were covered with brightly colored images of people and gods and creatures with the heads of animals and birds. Many household articles stood by the walls. He could see a table, two beautifully carved chairs, a few chests, several pitchers, and many other utensils. But only one set of objects gripped his heart as his eyes perceived them: weapons. Spears, superbly shaped bows, arrows, and daggers. A small altar of stone placed in the middle of a wall opposite the entrance sheltered a tall, dark opening in the wall behind it.

"I... Osiris Nerau-Ta, Scribe of the Temple of His Holiness, pray unto You, O Great Assembly of Gods, when on this day my heart is cast upon the scales—my heart, O mother of mine! my heart, O mother of mine!—may I pass along the road to fair judgment unhindered! Forsake me not in the presence of the One who wields the power..." Lauratas read out aloud, studying the wall of paintings. "Here is the tomb of Nerau-Ta, the Scribe... the one who died two months ago, the one who is to enter the place of rest before the great feast of the lake arrives. He was a man of great dignity. I would have heard of his body being committed to the tomb, but have not."

He uttered these words in a very low whisper and, taking the oil lamp with both hands, strode towards the dark opening. Whitehair followed him closely.

Beyond, they entered another chamber, a smaller one, the middle of which was occupied by a gigantic sarcophagus of shining red stone. Its lid was propped up against its side. A wooden stake placed between the lid and the wall protected it from sliding down and smashing. They looked inside. The sarcophagus was empty.

"They have not buried him yet. They intended to do so today or tomorrow. Look, they already gathered everything he will need in the world beyond. No one does this before the proper time arrives. Where are the guards? Have they run away? Have they perished in the storm?"

And saying no more, he lifted his lamp higher. Two small openings in the wall loomed out. He approached one and, ducking his head, vanished through the wall.

Whitehair followed. This chamber was narrow, and there was a small statue in the shape of a man standing on a small plinth, looking through a window painted on the wall. The other chamber contained an identical statue.

"They believe that the soul of the one who perishes from this earth dwells in these stone images," spoke Lauratas emerging from the passage.

He straightened up and looked about. Then he returned to the antechamber. Whitehair took hold of one of the pitchers standing by the wall and lifted it to his lips. "Water!" he cried, passing the pitcher to his companion. "Lauratas, water!"

And whilst the Cretan drank, he walked over to a huge bowl containing round pieces of hard bread. He lifted one of them to his lips. It was not fresh, but his teeth were sharp enough to break a piece off. And only now, as he chewed, did he notice how hungry he really was. After he ate his fill, he approached the weapons resting by the wall. He lifted one of the light spears, brandished it, and put it back.

Lauratas carefully placed the pitcher on the floor.

"Water! It has given me life and made my mind clear." But then he added in a lower tone: "Have the gods torn us out of the claws of the great wind and tossed us into this tomb so as to deny us a quick death in the wilderness and lead us back into the clutches of the priests of Sebek?"

"But why should our gods favor theirs?" asked the young Trojan.

"We are trespassing here. And remember, you killed the living effigy of god."

"Do you truly believe, Lauratas, that that fat and lazy crocodile was the living embodiment of a god? Would a true image of a god have submitted to me like a lamb? But tell me, what should we do?"

"As long as the storm persists, this tomb must serve for our shelter. But when the wind dies down, it will be time for us to force our way out and make our way for the swamp because we have no horses and therefore cannot hope to cross the desert and reach the river. But once we have reached the swamp, we can follow it north, enter the desert there and keep heading north until we reach the sea. Or until our pursuers find us."

"Do you believe that we have a chance of reaching the sea?"

"No, not really. But we have no other hope at all." Lauratas shrugged his shoulders.

But Whitehair detected a change in his voice, for though the Cretan had made a confession of doubt, his tone was no longer burdened with utter despair.

"Let us talk about this when the sandstorm has subsided. But if it is still raging, then we should probably rest and sleep. And the sooner we do so, the better."

And they placed themselves down on the cold, bare floor. Whitehair slipped his hand under his head and closed his eyes, but the veil of sleep would not descend upon him, for his mind dwelled on the question of what they would do once the storm passed.

Slowly, his thoughts evaporated into a mist, and in it, he saw himself standing on a rocky coast, witnessing a tiny fishing boat returning from the sea. And now he seemed to strain his eyes trying to see his father. But alas, the weather-beaten face was not there! Instead, the repulsive head of a crocodile adorned the sailor's shoulders, radiating a smile that grew wider as the boat drew nearer and then... it sank its teeth into Whitehair's flesh.

He struggled violently, trying to free himself.

"Wake up! Wake up!" a familiar voice floated through the darkness: it was Lauratas shaking him.

"Wake up!"

Whitehair sat up and rubbed his eyes, but only after he heard Lauratas speak again did he remember where he was.

"It is time to leave, we have slept too long. Come!"

Carefully, they walked along the corridor. But as soon as they got around the corner, they stopped with pounding hearts. The entire long and stony tunnel which led to the entrance was bathed in sunshine. Complete silence prevailed. The wind was gone.

"Gods have mercy!" whispered Lauratas. "It is day already!"

Quickly he moved towards the entrance, and falling upon his knees, he started to crawl. In no time, he was joined by Whitehair.

The morning sky was clear, and they could see the mountain-top at the opposite side of the ravine. It was a beautiful, quiet day.

A deep sleep must have kept them unconscious throughout the night.

They looked out carefully but immediately ducked back in.

A large procession was moving along the slope of the ravine, and it was pushing its way up the winding, stony road. A pair of priests led the way, followed by a few yokes of oxen with branching horns pulling a long sleigh. The mummy of Nerau-Ta, the scribe, destined to rest eternally, slept beneath its canopy. A woman, the wife of the resting one, followed close behind, digging her fingernails into her naked breast and drawing blood as she wept aloud. Then came the wailers, more priests, relatives, servants carrying gifts, and soldiers holding long spears.

But the procession stretched too far for Whitehair to see everyone at a glance.

They returned to the corridor and looked at one another.

"Will they enter this way?" breathed the young Trojan though the procession was still too far to hear their voices.

"I cannot say for sure, but I think so. It is the funeral of a great man, and no one as great as Nerau-Ta, the scribe, has died recently."

"Then we must run!" Whitehair turned towards the opening. "We must somehow slip away and run!"

"But the soldiers! Are you suggesting, wretched one, that we become fugitives on foot and scale these mountains?"

"What else can we do?" said the young Trojan in a trembling

voice. "They will catch us the moment they enter the tomb!"

Just then, the lament of the wailers reached their ears.

Whitehair remained still. His mind was tormented by a single thought: was it too late? Too late to run? To do anything to save themselves?

He offered no resistance when the Cretan took hold of his arm and led him down the corridor into the darkness towards the empty sarcophagus of Nerau-Ta, the scribe.

CHAPTER SEVEN
I Stand Before You

"They spoke to one of the peasants, and the older of the two enquired about the village to the west of the lake, close to its banks. But they were only trying to throw dust in our eyes, master, for they took water bags from him. Therefore, they intended to pass the mountains and cross the wilderness, making for the river."

The chief guard smiled a small, self-satisfied smile.

"Please, continue," said Het-Ka-Sebek trying to show no emotion.

"We would have pounced upon them by nightfall, master, but a great wind arose, and we had to seek shelter, for it is a force which all mortals must respect. Yet when it had passed, and we resumed our pursuit, my heart was filled with sorrow, for the gods were against us, and I knew that your most sacred command would not be carried out. For, in the midst of a storm like that, both man and beast are swept from the face of the earth unless the wilderness offers them some place of shelter. But the wind was so sudden and it came at a time when such storms are rare. Fear of your wrath, master, must have driven them into the wilderness, where the storm surely overcame them, for they could not have foreseen it coming or had time to find shelter. And so the only explanation is that heading east, they circled around the fertile lands, beyond the range of mountains, where the dead have their city. Our hounds scented one of their horses and the other a little later. Mountains of sand had built up in places where there had been none before, but fortunately for us, their horses were not buried deep down."

"You dug them up?"

"Yes."

"But what about the runaways?" asked Het-Ka-Sebek impatiently. "Speak of them!"

"One of the new mountains of sand must have undoubtedly claimed them, master, and there they will remain till the end of time. Their mortal remains must be a long way down, for our hounds could not smell them out."

"But can you be sure that they have found no shelter?"

"Master, I swear it! For we have searched the entire area. Without their horses, which probably threw them off during the sandstorm, they could not have gotten far. It stands to reason that they must have perished somewhere near their horses. The wind was so wild, master, that even the guards of the tomb of the venerable Nerau-Ta, the scribe, have perished. They left the tomb either in need of fresh air, or to satisfy a call of nature, or because they meant to flee the storm, and they were not spared but perished by falling to their doom. We found them beneath the sand at the bottom of the valley, and they were lifeless. Master, we searched the entire area. They could not have escaped. If they had hidden amongst the rocks, our hounds would have sought them out because we searched there also."

The priest looked at him carefully. He was aware that the man who had just spoken was a great hunter of men and that every one of his warriors knew each stone and crevice surrounding the city. And if the chief guard spoke with such unshaken conviction, he felt certain his words had to be true. This meant that both of them, the boy and the escaped slave, would not return to the temple alive. A most foul crime would not be avenged, for it seemed to Het-Ka-Sebek that even the cruelest death among the raging sands was but a small punishment for the bloody deed which the whitehaired boy had committed. It was an act of kindness for a sacrilegious murderer of god. But why should this happen? He did not know, for fathomless were the depths of thought which flowed in the minds of the gods.

"You may leave..." said the priest in a quiet and wearied voice.

The chief guard prostrated himself, rose, and bowing as he retreated backward, left the chamber. The Guardian of the Living Effigy of Sebek, the god sighed and, lost in thought, moved slowly towards the left wing of the great temple, where, at this time, he might hope to find the high priest. Let him decide how to proceed now that the immortal gods had sentenced the two malefactors to dwell in the sands for ever.

But as Het-Ka-Sebek walked, little did he know that the news of the fair-haired boy would reach his ears again. And it would reach them much sooner than he could have suspected.

Two priests, one dressed in white robes, the other in the skin of a leopard, led the funeral procession, followed by a yoke of oxen which pulled the mummy of Nerau-Ta, the scribe, resting inside a painted coffin upon a tall sleigh and shaded by a canopy. And behind, the wife of the scribe came wailing aloud and scratching her flesh with her fingernails, for this was the custom and the way of honoring the departed. Wailers, children, and grandchildren, trusted friends, armed guards, and servants carrying gifts for the tomb followed behind. And also two bulls: the Bull of the North, which was black, and the Bull of the South, which was white.

Gradually, advancing in a cloud of dust rising from their feet, the mourners reached the tomb and the dark entrance in the rock. They stopped.

Kher-Heb, the priest wearing the leopard skin, motioned with his hand, and now the two bulls were led forth in silence, broken only by the hollow sound of their hooves as they trampled the stones.

And when the other priest, called Sem, had smitten and slain the Bull of the North and the Bull of the South, he washed his hands in spring-water which was poured by a slave from a tall pitcher of alabaster, and bowed down solemnly before the tomb, greeting the gods of the Underworld. Now Kher-Heb burned incense, and the sons and trusted friends of the one who had departed heaved the coffin and set it upright so that once more Nerau-Ta, the scribe, could stand up straight and behold the land of the living.

Four times did Sem, the priest, read out the words of prayer from a scroll, during which Nerau-Ta, the scribe of the temple of his holiness, underwent the ritual of the Parting of the Lips, which Kher-Heb, the other priest, performed so that he could partake of food and utter words of defense in the Underworld when the gods decided to pass their judgment over him.

The two priests bowed down and walked into the depths of the tomb, followed by the slaves carrying the mummy upon their shoulders.

Again the groans and lamentations of the wailers arose, filling the stone corridor with echo, and the wife of Nerau-Ta, the scribe, fell down upon her knees, and crawled along and sprinkled her head with dust, which she had gathered from the ground with her hands.

And when they reached the large antechamber, Kher-Heb, the priest, approached the small stone altar and lifted his arms up high. All lamentations ceased.

"O, Osiris! Take upon Thyself, I beseech Thee, the sins of Nerau-Ta, the scribe!" cried out Kher-Heb, the priest, and Sem, the other priest, dipped his fingers in a silver vessel and splashed water of the Nile over the coffin of the departed with the likeness of Nerau-Ta, the scribe, painted upon its lid.

"O, Isis and Nephthys, mightiest sisters, and Thou, Thoth, who enters the acts of the mortals in the Scroll of Justice, have pity, and receive the remains of Nerau-Ta, the scribe, into the company of gods, so that he too may taste the bliss they enjoy, and together with them pass through Heaven and the Nether World in the Boat of Millions and Millions of Years..."

At times the melodious voice of Kher-Heb, the priest, rose, and at times it fell, as he uttered the words of the ritual four times, and Sem, the other priest, burnt incense again and sprinkled the altar with water, wine, and olive-oil and lifted pitchers of milk, beer, red and white wine from the ground, and placed them one by one upon the bier as the ceremony demanded, and also bowls containing copper, antimony, and iron. At last, he accepted a basket of onions and two white robes from the oldest son of Nerau-Ta, the scribe. And these he placed at the foot of the coffin.

In complete silence, surrounded by the flickering flames of torches, dimmed by the thickening smoke of the incense, which filled the entire chamber, Kher-Heb, the priest, uttered the final words of the ritual:

"Osiris Nerau-Ta, the scribe, the victorious, pronounces these words:

"'Glory to Thee, O Master, Wanderer of Eternity and Immortality! Glory to Thee, O Master of masters, O King of kings, O God of gods who abide by Thy side: I have come to Thee! Open before my eyes, I beseech Thee, the gates of Thy city, where those who adore the effigy of Thy Soul reside and let me mingle with those who will live for millions of years to come. Allow me, Osiris Nerau-Ta, the scribe, to enter and leave the Dark Kingdom at will. Allow me, I implore Thee, to be welcome in Thy city for all time to come.'"

And the arms of the priest froze in the air, his head dropped upon his shoulders, and he seemed lifeless. Only his ears remained open, for he listened for the sound of the soul of the dead Nerau-Ta, the scribe of the temple of his holiness, setting out on its journey into the Underworld. Undoubtedly, the ferocious god Anubis, with the head of a jackal, was even now preparing to snatch hold of the soul and bring it before the Great Assembly of Gods, who awaited his arrival in the Great Tribunal Chamber, anxious to see if the Quill of Truth would tip the Ultimate Scales.

At last, he lowered his arms. The widow lifted herself off her knees and placed a bunch of wild flowers upon the coffin. They had been picked beside the lake, where the scribe had often chosen to walk.

A hiss pierced the silence as the remains of the incense burned out in the earthenware holders.

Sem, the priest, made a sign. The bier shook a little and moved towards the burial chamber, where, with the greatest of care, the coffin was placed into the sarcophagus of stone. The slaves lifted the heavy stone lid and slid it onto the sarcophagus, sealing it shut. Now the priest placed down four urns in the four corners of the sarcophagus, containing the lungs, the stomach, the intestines, and the liver of Nerau-Ta, the scribe.

Then they stepped back in silence and looked upon the trusted friends of Nerau-Ta, the scribe, as they deposited upon the stone floor of the antechamber objects which would serve him in the Underworld and the small clay figures of *shabti* which would sow his seeds, plow his land, and execute each of his commands.

And, still in silence, the procession started leaving. Sem, the priest, and several slaves remained behind, and when the mourners had reached the winding road at the bottom of the valley, he gave the order to bring the oxen and carts of smoothly-hewn stones. Now, the slaves began to lay the blocks of rock deep inside the corridor and build a wall. And when it was finished, they sealed the entrance with enormous pieces of rock gathered earlier beside the opening.

And when all this work was completed, Sem, the priest, signaled once more.

A few slaves carrying ferruled rods climbed the almost perpendicular rock above the entrance. Keeping in rhythm with the soft song of their foreman, they thrust their poles into a deep, previously prepared fissure and began to swing them back and forth steadily.

Sem, the priest, moved back and, half-closing his eyes, carefully observed the crack in the rock. He shouted a sharp order. The poles stopped moving.

Then the priest shouted again.

The foreman leaned back against the rock whilst two slaves held him, and now he struck mightily with his stone hammer. They all jumped back and clung to the rock. But the block of stone remained unmoved. So the foreman struck a second time.

And now a deafening rumble reverberated in their ears as if the center of the rock had split. And for a while, the wall appeared to be motionless, but then the huge boulder fell down with a thud, and the entrance of the tomb was sealed for ever. A thick cloud of dust arose.

When the dust settled, Sem, the priest, nodded, for he was satisfied with what he saw and signaled to the slaves that their deed had been accomplished. The entrance of the tomb of Nerau-Ta, the scribe, had vanished for ever, and now no mortal on earth could disturb the perpetual peace of its occupant.

Without a word, the priest corrected the clasp of his robe and walked down. Some distance behind him walked the servant of the temple who was in charge of the slaves, and they, in turn, keeping a respectable distance, followed behind him in a crowd.

CHAPTER EIGHT
I Have Seen the Stars

Holding their breaths and keeping silent, they waited in their dark niches, hiding behind the statues of the dead scribe.

It was as if time had stopped. The incense stung their eyes, and suddenly Whitehair lost all hope of survival. But he gripped his dagger and waited. Should anyone approach and discover him or his friend, Lauratas, he would die fighting. Standing behind the statue, he could see nothing of what went on in the antechamber, but various sounds and voices told him that a great number of people had gathered there. They would enter here shortly and place the mummy at rest in its sarcophagus. And when that happened, only a true miracle could save them from being found crouching in the niches.

Then the slaves approached and placed the body into the sarcophagus. And as they lifted the lid of red stone, not one of them raised his eyes to look upon the fugitives, cloaked by the shadows of the niches. In silence, they retreated, and their steps faded down the corridor. A dreadful silence prevailed.

For a long time, they did not move, fearing greatly that someone had remained in the antechamber, either engrossed in prayer or fulfilling some final sacrifice.

The muffled crash of a falling boulder hit their ears from a distance, and this was followed by the grinding sound of many stones rolling over each other. Then they heard the voices of people from afar.

But still, they remained in their places, for they were

overcome with fear, and their eyes were almost blind with the smoke of the incense, and their bodies were suffering great pain.

Whitehair gritted his teeth, for he could no longer feel his legs and feared he would fall upon the ground.

Just then, the shadow of Lauratas appeared, barely visible in the light of the oil-lamps, which still shone through the entrance of the antechamber. Whitehair noticed his companion stealthily moving away from the wall and taking a few furtive steps toward the entrance.

The Cretan raised a hand in a warning sign, gripped a dagger, and signaled for the young Trojan to remain hidden. But Whitehair waited no longer and, stepping forth from his niche, began exercising his legs. He breathed heavily, keeping an eye on Lauratas, who crept along the wall and listened to the distant sounds in the corridor. Then he peered around the corner.

After a while, he beckoned to the young Trojan to come closer. Whitehair did so in silence.

"The incense, my friend, it must be put out, for otherwise, we shall suffocate and perish earlier than destiny has designed," whispered Lauratas. "The tomb is empty. We are alone. And the entrance, listen, it is being sealed with large stones."

The young Trojan tiptoed to the antechamber and, taking hold of one of the pitchers, poured several drops of wine onto the incense so that its flame hissed sadly and died. Now he looked round and placed the vessel upon the ground. Lauratas walked across the antechamber and stood listening in the corridor.

"But, tell me, is there anything we can do?" breathed Whitehair. "For if they finish and leave, shall we not be doomed for ever?"

"Only if we assailed them could we hope to see the light of day again. Still, we would not get far. The pursuit would soon be upon us, for in the entire region, I tell you, there are no trees, bushes, or caves that could offer us hiding. Why do you ask me such questions when you know the truth as well as I do? If we must perish here, a silent and tranquil death within the bounds of the tomb will be far kinder than the one we would suffer at the hands of the wrathful temple!"

"But every death is still a death?" said Whitehair instinctively. "What makes you speak of a better way to die? We still have time, and we must do what we can to save ourselves."

The Cretan quickly placed his hand upon the lips of his companion.

"Here we are safe from the eyes of the living..." he whispered into his ear. "We shall not perish in agony at once, for we still have some food and water. Yet..." He paused. The rumble of falling rocks ceased.

"Could they have finished their work... so quickly?" And taking the young Trojan by the hand, he walked along the corridor warily. As they reached the turn, they could still hear no sound.

Lauratas crouched down and looked around the corner. Complete darkness prevailed, and not a flicker of light came from the direction of the entrance.

Whitehair looked round.

"They have used huge rocks, but perhaps we can roll them aside after they depart... And if we free ourselves by nightfall, we can roll them back again and cover up our traces so that..."

A terrific crash shook the entire corridor. Something had happened outside.

"What was that?" the young Trojan staggered back and gripped his companion.

But the Cretan said nothing. Instead, he led him into the antechamber, which was full of burning oil-lamps, left behind by the mourners. And one by one, he extinguished them, leaving only one solitary lamp illuminating the walls. Then he turned round and said:

"I have blown them out so that they serve us longer."

But Whitehair looked towards the entrance of the tomb and breathed the same question:

"The sound we heard, I fear it betokens some great evil?"

The Cretan nodded in silence. After a while, he said: "There is enough food and drink here for at least a few days, and if we are careful, maybe a week. And there is plenty of olive-oil too. Let us thank the gods that Nerau-Ta, the scribe, was a wealthy man, for he has been furnished with everything he needed on his way. But what shall we tell him when we ourselves cross the threshold to the Shades? He will accuse us in the presence of his gods of pillaging his tomb and of taking his possessions!"

He tried to smile but only creased his face instead.

"You ask what it was? There is a custom here of sealing tombs so as to protect them from robbers. Just look at these vessels and ornaments of gold littering the ground. For a pauper, they would be a pass to a better life, and such a person would be willing to risk his own vile existence to break in here and plunder them. But it is the solemn belief of all Egyptians that their life possessions must accompany them into the next world. Therefore those who are wealthy enough secure their fates after death by building tombs in the ground and filling them with riches. I was deluding myself into thinking that having blocked the tomb with huge rocks, they would return another day to seal it properly, but they had made a crack in the side of the mountain much earlier, meaning to force a piece of it to drop over the entrance, thus preventing anyone from getting in. And if my ears have not deceived me, we have been trapped by a boulder of prodigious size. It would take hundreds of slaves with equipment and draught animals to move such an enormous weight."

Whitehair started up from the stone floor at the foot of the altar. He looked into the eyes of the Cretan, barely visible in the gloom, and whispered:

"Are we then... buried alive?"

Lauratas nodded in silence and shrugged his shoulders.

"I have said what I know. It is better to perish here than to feel the clutches of Het-Ka-Sebek. For, whatever happens, the god of the lake cannot reach us here."

"Are you willing to sit here and do nothing while we finish

our nourishment and watch the oil in our lamps burn out so that we may be spared the sight of our own torture?"

"No. I am ready to fight to the very end. But we must wait a little, for the slaves could still be covering the traces leading to the tomb. We shall go to the entrance later and see what stands between us and the world of the living. Whatever happens, we must free ourselves. We cannot leave now. Therefore let us search this place, for it may contain things of use to us."

And they started inspecting both chambers, lifting objects, placing them back again, and gathering all the food and drink in one corner so that they would know exactly how much was left.

"There is an abundance of olive-oil. And it will serve two purposes, for it will give light to our lamps and nourishment to our bodies with its pleasant taste and greasy flavor. However, our water and wine supplies are low. We need not worry too much about that, for the tomb is quite cool. Therefore, if I had no fear of the wrathful gods, I would say that we could probably survive here for twenty days. But let us be hopeful that we shall be able to find an opening for ourselves."

"And if at first, it is small, we shall soon make it larger. But come, Lauratas, we must see what the slaves have done, for otherwise, we shall never know what the gods have decided."

The Cretan took hold of a long, heavy spear lying by the altar and also lifted the smallest of the oil-lamps.

"Choose a few short daggers..." said he, looking down at the weapons, "short daggers with wide blades. We shall try to lever the stones."

They entered the corridor, illuminated dimly by the lamp which flickered in the hand of the Cretan. The young Trojan looked down the corridor, and it appeared to be a lot shorter now. Even the slightest ray of sunlight did not penetrate the mighty wall of large, rectangular rocks built by the slaves.

They approached slowly and stopped. Lauratas lifted his lamp in an attempt to illuminate the entire wall with its light. The blocks of stone were piled up evenly, one on top of the other, and were so smooth that they fitted exactly, forming a wall. Just below the ceiling, they noticed that many small rocks had been forced in so as to seal the small spaces between the wall and the ceiling.

"They were in a hurry..." murmured Lauratas. "We may be hopeful. These stones are not too big for us to move. And look, they have used neither clay nor mortar to hold them together. It is strange, for normally Egyptians attach great importance to the safety of their tombs, particularly when wealthy people, such as Nerau-Ta, the scribe, pay the debt of nature. Therefore we must be prepared to face another obstacle behind this one, for the one before us cannot defy us successfully."

"Then let us find out what really locks us in!"

But the Cretan did not answer and walked up to the barrier of stone, lifting his lamp and contemplating its surface.

"There could be a space behind this wall..." said Whitehair uncertainly. "Therefore, it is not worth our time and energy to take it all apart. If we remove just a few stones, I shall slip through and investigate further."

"I heard them throw a great number of loose rocks. And the sound they produced was muffled. It is more than likely that there is a pile of rubble beyond this wall. But then the entrance itself, my friend, is probably sealed in some way. If we can push one of these stones at the top, we shall be able to find out how things stand."

Whitehair slipped the blade of his dagger into a gap between two pieces of hewn rock and pulled lightly. The stone moved a little.

"Look, Lauratas, they are loose!" He removed his dagger and pulled again.

The Cretan put his lamp down and, carefully thrusting the head of his spear into the slit, began moving the rock about gradually. And gradually, the rectangular and smooth block of stone emerged from its slot. When one of its sides entirely came forward, the young Trojan let the dagger fall to the ground and grasped the stone with both hands. Then he pulled it out slowly, and it offered no resistance but swung around obediently. Together with Lauratas, who gripped it from the bottom, they managed to take it out completely and place it down by the wall.

A few tiny rocks fell out of the dark hole. Lauratas lifted his oil-lamp and, holding their breaths, they peered inside.

"They have done just as I believed they would. The corridor has been blocked not only by a wall but also by a heap of rubble. We must clear everything away if we wish to see the light of day again. A great amount of work awaits us, for they have collected many stones from the ravine and have not had to transport them far."

"But there is something strange in all this, Lauratas. Or could this be all they have done? Surely a few thieves could easily break into a tomb protected like this."

"You have forgotten about the great rumble which we heard at the end. Nothing we see here could have created such a crash. I have told you, they are not such fools as to seal the entrance without thought. We must take this wall apart and clear the corridor, and then we shall see what really imprisons us. Bring another lamp."

And in silence, they got down to work, trying to make as little noise as possible, for despite the solitude of the necropolis, they feared that the relatives of the scribe might return to offer up prayers before the tomb.

Hardly resting, they removed the barrier of stone blocks and set about removing the rubble, which they placed beside the wall of the corridor.

The entrance was much closer now. But they were unconscious of the passage of time, and when one of the oil-lamps went out, they hardly seemed to notice, for their eyes had grown so accustomed to the gloom that they could work equally well in the poorest of light. But when the second lamp flickered with a long flame and died, the corridor was plunged into absolute darkness, and now Lauratas leaned back against the rocks and breathed in deeply.

"It was a large lamp. A lamp like that might burn throughout the night or even longer," said the Cretan wearily. "Could we have worked that long?"

Whitehair wiped his eyes, for they were full of dust, and immediately a weakness ran through his body.

"Let us nourish ourselves, Lauratas... and return to our task without delay..." he whispered, moving his stiff fingers.

And so, groping in the dark, they returned to the antechamber, where Lauratas kindled a light.

"This custom of offering a basket of onions to the departed one is most fitting," he said almost cheerfully as he emptied the contents of the bag and inspected the onions with the greatest of care. "They have been chosen carefully. And they will remain succulent for a long time and will not rot. Eat!"

He placed a few onions and a large piece of dry bread beside the boy.

"But remember, restrain yourself from drinking too much water, for we shall perish once there is none!"

They nourished themselves in silence, and when their hunger was sated, they took a few sips of water, and the whitehaired Trojan sat down and looked towards his companion.

"How much time could have passed, Lauratas, since we first entered the tomb?"

"The gods alone can say. But ask them how much longer we must remain here, for this undoubtedly is of greater importance."

"We shall never know if we continually rest..."

Whitehair struggled to his feet, taking hold of a lamp.

"You speak wisely..." yawned the Cretan, wiping his wearied eyes. "We must learn what cuts us off from the land of the living."

And again, they worked in silence, gasping for air, for the stones they had been lifting with considerable ease now seemed incredibly heavy.

At last, a black gap appeared above the rubble.

The Cretan wiped the sweat from his eyes and climbed up on his toes, almost touching the roof of the corridor.

"There is darkness beyond..." he whispered. "I see no stones there."

Their hearts pounded as they hurled pieces of rock over their shoulders so as to increase the size of the gap. At last, they rolled away a huge boulder that remained in their way and stepped forward with their lamps.

A short section of the corridor stretched beyond the rubble and a little further on...

"Great gods!..." breathed the young Trojan. "The mountain has collapsed upon us!"

Indeed, an almost smooth and uniform wall of rock stood in their way, blocking it completely.

Lauratas raised his lamp to illuminate the dreadful sight. But when he spoke, his voice was calm.

"I could have foretold this. But let us be thankful to the gods that the air we breathe here is much clearer than yonder in the depths of the tomb. Here we shall not suffocate. And once we find our way beyond this gigantic rock... nothing will hinder our way into the Valley of the Dead."

Whitehair walked up to the obstacle and touched its surface. Then he leaned his shoulder against it in a desperate and hopeless effort to push it away.

"Why do you squander your strength on such a futile task? A hundred men could not accomplish what you hope to achieve. It is beyond our might, for we can neither pierce it nor roll it away..."

"What can we do?"

"If we wish to get out of here, there is only one thing to do, and that is to dig a tunnel beneath the rock. Do you see another way out?"

"Then let us busy ourselves, Lauratas..."

The young Trojan looked about and, kneeling down, touched the ground.

"Think more wisely, son of a fisherman! For if we do not rest now, we shall have no strength to scrape a hole beneath the boulder with the tools we possess and then to climb out."

Whitehair looked at the smooth, dull rock with indecision and whispered:

"Yes, Lauratas, we must rest." And he followed the Cretan. When they reached the burial chamber, he lay down, leaning his head against the corner of the altar, and fell asleep at once.

When they woke, they walked up the corridor and worked without rest until their hands could serve them no longer, after which they returned to nourish themselves and to sleep a little, but in no time at all, they were standing upon the stone floor again, lighting their lamps and returning to the place, where the infinitely stubborn and solid boulder surrendered only bit by bit.

They had no sense of time. Whitehair tried to count the passage of days, but he was not sure whether he had risen from his sleep ten times or possibly twenty. Many days could have passed outside, but maybe not as many as he thought. He sighed. What could it all mean? Their lives were not measured in days but by the thickness of the rock under which they were forced to dig.

He fell asleep again.

When he awoke, he could not remember where he was. Utter and impenetrable darkness embraced him, absorbing the remains of his dream. He had dreamed of a ship sailing upon the vast blue calm of the sea. But it was empty, for he did not see the rowers upon their thwarts, nor indeed the steersman with his steering oar. A gentle wind swelled the purple sail with strange figures and symbols similar to the pictures on the walls of the tomb of Nerau-Ta, the scribe.

He shook his head. But the darkness persisted. A steady, soft sound reached his ears. Lauratas was sleeping close by.

Whitehair closed his eyes. And now, a new wave of sleep swept over his body, but with an effort, he opened his eyes again. He had grown accustomed to the darkness, for they now used their lamps only when they worked. Two pitchers, one of water and one of wine, were all that they had left to drink. The water was losing its freshness, and the wine, though it quenched their thirst, deprived them of the strength to work. Fighting the pain which tormented his entire body, he heaved himself onto his elbow and sat up, leaning against the wall of the antechamber where they slept, for they seemed to fear the thought of living in the burial chamber, where the scribe rested in his stone sarcophagus.

He placed his left hand upon his lips and could feel that his fingers were covered in painful sores, but he tried not to think about them, knowing that they would only get worse each time he returned to work.

Using pieces of stone as hammers, they would strike the hilts of their blunt daggers laboriously so that little chips of rock, and sometimes no more than a few grains of sand, would fall away as they bore laboriously below the foot of the boulder. Their work crawled along, but they wasted no time, for whenever one exhausted his strength and could hold his tool no longer, the other was ready to take his place. And so the opening increased in size until at last, they managed to carve a hollow beneath the huge rock large enough for a man to crawl under. But they could not say how thick this towering boulder was and knew not how much longer they would have to dig.

When they had gone for their last rest, the hollow was already deep, and it ran a long way beneath the rock. But every moment was marked with increasing difficulty, for now, there was even less room in which to work.

"Lauratas!" said Whitehair in a low voice.

The sound of soft breathing stopped, and in its place, a quiet sigh could be heard, followed by the voice of the Cretan who had woken up.

"I had a dream about our rock, that we had dug our way through, and that we beheld the starry heavens above the mountains. There was no moon, only the stars, a vast number of them, so vast that I thought the gods must have been sowing them incessantly during our stay underground."

"May your dream come true today!"

A quiet scratching sound reached his ears, and then a light flashed, unveiling the paintings on the stone walls of the small chamber, which to Whitehair appeared to be so familiar as if he had dwelled here from the day of his birth.

They rose. Lauratas wiped his eyes and straightened up. Two deeply sunken eyes shone in his grimy, dusty face.

"And even if we do see the stars above..." murmured he walking along the corridor. "We will be doomed all the same, like that ill-fated creature who cuts the rope around his neck, only to find himself falling down into the precipice below."

"We have stayed here so long," spoke the young Trojan with unshaken confidence, "that they must have pronounced us dead by now. Only fools could think that the storm did not devour us. But, tell me, how long have we been prisoners here? It must be ten or maybe even twenty days in all."

"Yes, maybe ten days have passed..." Lauratas shrugged his shoulders. "Or maybe twice that number. It shall remain a mystery to us, for we shall speak to no one, and there will be no way of finding out."

The Cretan stopped in front of the solid wall of rock obstructing the corridor and, looking upon Whitehair, tried to smile.

"Will the light of day or the shadow of night greet us when at last we return to the world of the living?"

"Let it be the light of day, for darkness has served its time, and it will be fitting to see the rays of the sun. But thoughts such as these have no place in my mind."

"What is it that troubles you?"

"Many days have passed since the waters of the lake rose. And had I not slain that monster, it would have ripped me apart and devoured me long ago. Therefore, whatever may happen, I know I have done well to shed its blood."

He looked at the Cretan, who had kneeled down and placed an oil-lamp beside the hollow they had dug in preparation to slip under the rock.

"But you, Lauratas, would still be living safely in the temple of Sebek, and no one would be hunting you like a wild animal, nor would you be cut off from the world by this wall of rock—if it had not been for me."

"Matters such as these should not be spoken of," Lauratas shook his head reluctantly. "For we are mere mortals, and it is the gods who govern our fates. For all I know, they may have brought you to Egypt in order to lead me out of it and to take me back to the land of my fathers before I die. Alone, I would have never found enough courage in my heart to run. And what good are a few more years of life, or even many, if I am to remain a slave till my dying day? A foreign land would claim my remains, and I would be thrown into a hole by the side of another slave. We are ignorant of the future, for when you slew their god, it seemed that we would be caught by nightfall. I was convinced of this, yet many days and nights have passed, and we are still alive. And though we are confined to this tomb, we are masters of ourselves, and for years I have not tasted this kind of freedom. Pass me my dagger."

He slipped his head under the rock and then his shoulders. Gradually he pushed down further whilst Whitehair held the lamp just above the ground and, enveloped in almost complete darkness, tried to light the way for the Cretan.

He could hear him hammering away with the piece of stone and dagger. Then his muffled voice sounded:

"The echo in the rock sounds different."

There was a moment of silence.

More hammering.

Then silence again.

Whitehair waited anxiously, holding the lamp near the hollow. The flame started flickering. Fortunately, there were a few tiny chinks and irregularities between the side of the mountain and the giant boulder they could drill into. A few more light hammerings.

Silence again.

"What is it, Lauratas?" he whispered.

But the Cretan did not answer.

After a while, his bare feet appeared, then his legs, and at last, he emerged entirely and sat down by the hollow. The young Trojan was about to speak but stopped, for Lauratas lifted his hand to his lips, holding his dagger. Then he nodded. Whitehair placed the lamp down and looked towards the hollow. And still not speaking, Lauratas nodded again. He rose and, leaning towards his companion, whispered into his ear:

"Already... I have seen the stars... but with one eye only, for the hole is still very small."

He drew a deep breath and wiped the sweat from his forehead, which had appeared in large drops, though he had not been working for long. Closing his eyes, he said:

"Go and see for yourself..."

The young Trojan vanished under the boulder. But he could see nothing, and the darkness was as thick as in the rest of the tomb. Feverishly he groped about with his fingers, trying to find the hole. At last, he located it and pressed his face against the cold rock.

"I see them..." he said. "Lauratas! I see them! And the top of the mountain facing us! And the stars above, one... two... three... five, many! Lauratas! It is true! I see them! Pass me my dagger!"

He crawled back without turning round and stretched out his hand for his tool.

"Wait!" said the Cretan. "Come back out to me!"

Reluctantly the young Trojan reappeared. His heart was pounding.

"Why do you stop me? Surely this is the time to dig! We must use the cover of night and free ourselves before the dawn of a new day."

"Undoubtedly, but first, we must gather everything we need. Let us bring our nourishment and weapons and set them down somewhere near so that when the hole is large enough, we can leave without delay."

They retreated to the antechamber and lit nearly all of the oil-lamps, but this dazzled their eyes, for they had grown quite unaccustomed to such intensive light.

Whitehair walked up to the pile of weapons.

"What about these spears?"

"We shall leave them, for, without horses, we must carry everything ourselves. But these bows will be of more use to us for hunting wild animals or beating off our enemies, should they appear."

A few daggers remained. Whitehair chose one: it was long and thin, and precious stones had been set in its hilt. Then he touched his breast instinctively, brushing a finger over his only memento of his native Troy. The dagger was still in its goatskin sheath, dangling from his neck. He slipped the second one into a quiver full of arrows and took hold of a small bow, its dark wood inlaid with bits of silver forming strange inscriptions, and now he looked about with indecision.

"There is some grain in the bowls, Lauratas. And we still have a few onions. Do you intend to take them with you?"

"We must take the onions, for we do not know when we shall have the good fortune to find something to eat. If the gods lead us out of the Valley of the Dead, it will be wise to make haste for the sea of reeds growing along the river beyond the mountains, to the east. Then we must steal a fisherman's boat and head for the sea by night. But when the day comes, we must retire to the marshes and sleep with birds and crocodiles. Many people live along the banks of the great river, and their dwellings stretch as far as the sea. And if but one of the peasants should see us, word of our existence would go abroad. But the closer we get to the estuary of the river, the wider and more extensive it will become, dividing into many arms which push towards the sea. Therefore, if we pass the great cities in the depths of night, I tell you, with the help of the gods, we shall be guided to the sea itself."

"And then?"

"And then we shall know that the great sea alone stands between us and our native land. You yourself were born beside the sea, and as you have said, it gives life to your people, as does soil or craftsmanship to others. But I, too, am the son of islanders, whose ships wander the seas, and I have no fear of the sea, nor do I stand in awe when Poseidon shows his anger. Besides, since the day you slew that monster, I have come to believe that every death is better than the one which the priests of Sebek would devise for the two of us."

He touched the young Trojan's shoulder. "Remember, we cannot be caught alive, for there can be nothing worse than that fate for us!"

Whitehair nodded silently and reached for a white sacrificial garment, ripped it apart, and, tying a bundle out of its shreds, filled it with the remaining onions.

"I am ready, Lauratas."

The Cretan, also armed with a bow and long dagger, walked up to the altar, where a disarray of objects belonging to Nerau-Ta, the scribe, lay in a heap. He rummaged about for a while until, at last, he found what he was looking for,

"Take these two gold chains. They are beautiful and have been made with great skill. Put them around your neck or into the bundle you have made. And this ring, too: it has the shape of their holy beetle and is carved in a very precious, sky-blue stone which comes to this land from very far away. These people value such rings very highly, and one of them is worth the price of a few young and healthy slaves."

"But what good are they to us? We cannot buy slaves, Lauratas!"

"Take them! Let each of us take a little tinsel. Nothing surpasses the predominance of gold, for it will deliver us from peril, and neither the most elaborate words nor indeed beseechings of the greatest despair can be more eloquent. And here we stand, ignorant of the many mysteries lying ahead of us on our journey."

Reluctantly Whitehair untied the bundle, put the necklace in, and slipped the ring onto his finger.

"I have done as your wisdom has commanded, Lauratas, but let us be gone, for we do not know how old the night was when we first looked up to the stars, and remember, only those out of their senses would dare to try their escape in daylight. There are no trees and bushes around here."

They walked towards the opening, and when they stopped, Lauratas placed a finger upon his lips.

"It is night, and the thud of our hammering against the boulder will spread far and wide." He shook his head. "But there is nothing we can do about this. I shall wrap a rag around the stone and the hilt of my dagger. It shall muffle the noise a little."

He slipped into the hollow, and after a while, a muffled knocking could be heard.

The Cretan worked quickly and tirelessly. Then he withdrew a little and started throwing tiny pieces of rock into the corridor.

Then he reached deeper down and triumphantly produced a huge piece of rock, freshly broken from the boulder.

"A part of the boulder must have crumbled when I struck it, and this piece fell away on its own. I fear that some of its fragments could drop from the outside and tumble down the mountain, filling the entire valley with its echo..." He was very tired and gasped for air, but there was a smile on his lips. "There is no moon, and though the sky is full of stars, it is a very dark night. And the opening is almost big enough. I have stretched my hand through and touched the world of the living!"

"Let me go and take my turn, Lauratas. For I sit here with folded arms..."

"No!" The Cretan shook his head in stern refusal. "You are young and overhasty. Just one thoughtless movement, and you could bring the enemy upon us. And anyone who belongs to the temple is an enemy! Therefore wait here and be patient!"

He returned to his work while Whitehair reached for the pitcher and swallowed a few mouthfuls of water. But it was so fusty that he shuddered in disgust and sat listening in the hollow.

At last, Lauratas appeared.

"The opening is large enough for my head to get through!"

he whispered. "But my shoulders are still too wide. Yet as I look upon your body, I see that you could easily crawl through to the outside. Do so, and I shall hand you our possessions. Place them by the rock and lie down and let your ears be attentive, for, at times, the desert guards ride past, looking for tomb robbers. And should they happen to be close by and hear us, we would bitterly regret ever starting to dig this hole."

"Yes, Lauratas."

He vanished beneath the boulder. The hole was not very large, but he did manage to thrust himself through, even though its jagged edges ripped his skin.

For a while, the young Trojan lay still, gazing up at the stars in the sky and breathing in deeply the fresh, clean air of the night. He felt a lump in his throat. But just then, an almost soundless whisper floated across to him:

"Here!"

A hand appeared holding a bundle. Whitehair took the parcels and weapons and placed them a few paces from the boulder. Then he put one of the bows onto his shoulder and slung a quiver of arrows across his chest. At once, he returned to the boulder.

And only now did he realize what a colossal rock the slaves had pushed against the entrance. The tremendous crash had caused it to crack in a few places. Just above the spot where Lauratas had bored the hole, a deep fissure was showing.

"Had we known," he thought, "our freedom would have come much earlier."

He walked away and sat down, listening. The entire valley and surrounding mountains, rocky and rugged, were filled with the deepest silence. Not a sound, not even the slightest breath of wind.

"Do you hear anything?" whispered Lauratas.

"No," said Whitehair, returning to the boulder. "The night is black, and as I look to the east, I cannot see the coming of day. Night must have fallen just as you first pierced through the rock."

"We are fortunate…" said the Cretan breathlessly and stirred.

He was checking how much more rock had to be smashed away.

"I will strike it here..." And he stretched forth his hand out of the hole and pointed to a bulge on its upper edge. "For I see a crack in the rock, and it will crumble with greater ease."

The young Trojan stepped back, for he wished to look at the boulder and see how far the crack had reached. But just then, the Cretan struck the bulge with all his might.

The rock seemed to utter a groan. Whitehair wanted to shout and throw himself onto the boulder, but instead, he remained frozen. He could see nothing but the hand of Lauratas looming out of the hole as if it were fighting in desperation to leave the tomb.

And suddenly, the huge mass of rock slipped down a little and came to rest without making any further sound. A tiny cloud of dust blew out of the hole.

At first, Whitehair did not realize what had happened. Trembling, he approached the boulder. The opening was no longer there, and in its place, an enormous hunk of loose rock had settled, and the mountainside looked the same as when he had first stepped out of the tomb.

But it was not the mass of rock that absorbed the Trojan, for he was staring at something else which shone beneath the boulder, illuminated by the gloomy twinkle of stars, and it filled his eyes with horror.

The fingers of a mortal were gripping the ground beneath the edge of the boulder.

"Lauratas..." he whispered. "Lauratas .."

He stepped forward and looked. At once, he knew he could do nothing. Lauratas would never see his native shores again. There he lay, crushed by the huge mass of rock, like an ant that perishes beneath the foot of a human, ignorant of its impending fate. So close to freedom and yet lost for ever.

The young Trojan quickly gathered many small stones and placed them with great care over the fingers of his lost friend. Then he built a little mound from the soil and fortified it with a few rocks so that neither hyena nor carrion-feeding bird could violate Lauratas's hand.

He rose and wiped his eyes. And now, the night in the Valley of the Dead was his only companion.

"I must depart now, Lauratas," he breathed.

He straightened up and, clenching his fist, touched his forehead as a sign of homage.

"I must depart, but if ever I set foot on your native shore, I swear to light an offering to the immortal gods so that your soul will enjoy peace in the land of shadows."

Again he wiped his eyes with his naked forearm and walked towards the precipice where he had left the bundles. Biting his lip, he took the arrows which had belonged to Lauratas and placed them into his quiver, then he took his bow and laid it down by the boulder. Then he added Lauratas's onions to his own bundle, but the golden earrings and bangles which the Cretan had chosen for himself, he tossed away.

Once more, he cast his eyes back toward the boulder. And now he looked at the mountain ridge, but the night was still too young to be swept aside by the light of day.

He was about to leave but stopped suddenly and slipped back in silence, gently pressing against the boulder. Carefully he set down his bundle and, taking out an arrow, slipped his bow off his shoulder. Down in the valley, a piece of rock had rattled.

Then another. And now he strained his eyes, scanning the grey mountains in order to see what it was that lurked amongst them.

He waited. An intense silence filled the valley once more. Again a rock rolled down, still closer.

At last, the stars revealed the solitary figure of a man on horseback.

He was trotting along the winding, stony road, pushing his way up. Undoubtedly he was one of the desert guards patrolling the Valley of the Dead in order to keep away any tomb raiders. If this was so, then many more of them must be close at hand, for it would be foolish for anyone to venture into these mountains alone.

The rider trotted along slowly, but every step drew him nearer. Clearly, he believed himself to be alone, for he betrayed no caution. Possibly he had wandered these secluded spots throughout the night and was now returning to his people. Shortly he would pass by the tomb of Nerau-Ta, the scribe.

Whitehair looked about quickly. A steep wall of the mountain towered above him, and to reach the valley below, he would have to cross an open stretch of the rocky mountainside, and this he could not do, for anyone could see him from a distance, even by starlight. And there was no way back. But if he and the guard met, one of them would surely pay the penalty of death.

"The horse!" it flashed through his mind. Distinctly now, he could hear each hoof beating against the rocks.

The rider had stopped climbing the winding trail, for he had already reached the height of the tomb of the scribe. His dark shape stood out clearly against the night sky. In one of his hands, he held a short spear, and in the other, probably the reins of his horse.

"He will let his beast rest a little, for it has climbed a long way, and then he will spur it on," thought the young Trojan.

He was very close now. The horse snorted and tossed its head, for it had sensed the presence of a stranger among the rocks.

The rider stopped. A profound silence fell, and Whitehair looked at the spear the guard held, but its blade had vanished. Surely the rider must have lowered it.

He did not even realize when he released his arrow. He heard a short whistle and jumped forward.

The horse reared, and the body of the rider rolled onto the ground. Many rocks rattled down the slopes.

Whitehair grasped the horse's reins and hung onto them so that the horse could toss its head no more. But it continued to rear desperately, and only after a while did it settle down, snorting heavily.

Holding the copper bit in his right hand, the young Trojan

leaned back, snatched his bundles from the ground, and jumped onto the horse.

And now the beast leaped about just above the precipice. He held the reins with all his might and battled the horse, forcing its head down. Suddenly he released his hold and bent forward low, embracing its neck.

The horse galloped along the narrow trail, above the precipice, towards the pass between the mountains.

Whitehair recognized this place at once, for it was here that the great wind had caught them. And it was here also that he, Whitehair, had pushed forward towards the valley with unseeing eyes, sure of doom, and only the helpful hand of Lauratas had delivered him from peril and led him into the tomb of Nerau-Ta, the scribe.

He shuddered at the thought of that same hand, lifeless, crushed beneath the boulder.

He reached the mountain-pass and stopped. The horse was panting heavily.

To the east, the sky was turning grey. The Trojan looked about, and the words of his lost friend sounded in his mind:

"Make haste for the sea of reeds growing along the river beyond the mountains... Take a small boat and head for the sea by night."

"And so it shall be, Lauratas!" he said.

He slapped his horse with an open palm and turned right toward the east, where, hidden in the distance and the night, the great river rolled along in turbid, silty waves, slithering on towards the far-off sea.

CHAPTER NINE
If You Do Not Find Him, Ants Will Devour You

Het-Ka-Sebek, Peace Guardian of the Living Effigy of the Soul of Sebek, the god, sat in his litter with a thin purple canopy above him. He looked at an army of slaves, who had tied strong lines round the top of the boulder blocking the entrance to the tomb of Nerau-Ta, the scribe of the temple of his holiness.

The slaves worked quickly, for the sun had just passed the zenith and now blazed over the valley filling it with such a great heat that they found it difficult to tread upon the burning rocks with their bare feet.

And once again, Het-Ka-Sebek lifted the arrow in his hand and saw that its shiny point of gilded bronze was stained black with blood. The body of the desert guard lay lifeless beside the entrance, away from the eyes of the priest.

"Nerau-Ta," he read for the hundredth time and for the hundredth time, he shook his head in disbelief, never before so close to fear. The wife of the scribe, his children, and all of the relatives who had taken part in the funeral rituals swore by the almighty gods that this arrow had been placed in the tomb along with all the others. As was the bow which the desert guards had found close by.

But it was strange that the gold bodkins and earrings should lay scattered upon the ground as if the pillagers of the tomb had found no value in them. Possibly the guard had surprised them so that they dropped some of their spoils and later could not find them in the dark and fled for fear of more guards and their hounds.

Now he lifted the curtain on the right side of the litter and looked down into the valley, where several horses stood together, guarded by two swarthy and half-naked riders. Others were wandering about the mountainside with their hounds, searching for tracks. A white headdress shone in the sun, and he recognized Haugha, the chief of the desert guards.

Then he looked at the boulder which closed the tomb. And he shook his head. Why, at a time when the heat of the day is at its greatest and when only absolute necessity drives people out of their dwellings, did he, Het-Ka-Sebek, decide to undertake such a toilsome journey?

He thought of his god, who had not yet been avenged. And yet he knew that the fugitives had perished in the desert, for fully twenty days had passed, and no one could survive so long without help in the desolate mountains beyond the city. And Het-Ka-Sebek was convinced that the perpetrators of the sacrilege would have received assistance from no one.

He signaled to the slave who was fanning him to stop and emerged from the litter, using the back of another slave as a platform upon which to place his feet. Slowly, the priest walked up to the boulder and leaned upon his golden staff. A sudden shout from a priest in charge of the workers sounded in his ears, and the slaves heaved mightily and then heaved again. Over a hundred men were straining at the ropes. Het-Ka-Sebek watched their backs grow tense with exertion. He waited. The mass of the rock trembled and leaned forward a little but refused to fall any further and then leaned back again with a tremendous thud. The ground beneath their feet shuddered. Again the priest shouted, and again the slaves heaved. And once more, they relaxed their hold.

For a moment, the boulder remained motionless as if deliberating which direction to take. But at last, it leaned away from the mountainside and slowly tumbled over. As it did so, a deafening rumble filled the air, huge pieces of rock rolled down into the valley, and a thick cloud of red dust arose and veiled the tomb.

But Het-Ka-Sebek remained where he was, calm and motionless, and when the boulder began to shatter, only he did not stir, whilst everyone else stepped back in awe.

The veil of dust slowly settled.

Walking at a steady, even pace, the tall priest approached the entrance of the tomb.

He paused and looked down. Then he signaled to the others, who were standing at a distance, too frightened to approach without his orders.

"What is this?" said the priest. "The remains of a mortal?"

"Yes, O most venerable master! He must have perished beneath the boulder, and when the boulder moved again, the rest of his body was torn apart. It will be difficult to recognize him."

Het-Ka-Sebek bit his lip. It was indeed a frightful sight. But despite this, he stepped forth and, standing over the crushed body, peered into the depths of the dark corridor. And he stood there for some time, engrossed deep in thought. Then he beckoned the priests who had committed the mummy of Nerau-Ta, the scribe, to the tomb.

"Tell me, my brothers, which of you was present at the sealing of the tomb?"

"I was, O Het-Ka-Sebek, Peace Guardian of the Living Effigy of the Soul of Sebek, the god!" said Sem and stepped forth.

"Tell me, Sem, did any one of your slaves meet his death at the entrance to the tomb? Was there one who fell victim to the boulder?"

"No. They all returned."

The eyes of the priest wandered down and observed the dreadfully mutilated body.

"And did you see to it that the corridor leading to the chambers was walled off and filled with stones?"

"I did, O most venerable Guardian!"

Het-Ka-Sebek asked no more questions, and now he stepped forward into the tomb, beckoning Sem to follow. They passed the heap of rubble, which clearly had been disturbed, and stopped before the demolished wall.

"Give me light!" spoke Het-Ka-Sebek. "And let the slaves clear the corridor!"

And only after they had brought torches and carried out his orders did he choose to move on. A great many priests were gathered at the entrance, but not one of them spoke as they peered into the darkness of the tomb and at the mortal remains on the ground.

Het-Ka-Sebek did not emerge from the tomb for a long time, but when he finally did, followed by Sem, everyone looked upon his face and saw that he was greatly perturbed.

"Which of you can tell me the color of the hair of the slave from the People of the Sea, who escaped from our temple together with the one who dared to strike our god?"

A few of the people stepped forward.

"Look this way and let your memories be sharp!" He indicated the body by the entrance.

"It is the same as that of the slave called Lauratas!" spoke one of them, and another of the onlookers bore him out.

"Yes! I also recognize him. Many a time did I see him during the journey which I undertook along the river in order to bring back the whitehaired offering. But this is no ordinary affair. Let the chief of the desert guards place himself before me."

And soon, the swarthy warrior appeared running along the mountainside, after which he threw his white headdress off and fell upon his knees, leaning his head towards the ground beside the golden sandals of the priest. Het-Ka-Sebek, still looking down, spoke these words:

"You pledged your life, Haugha, that the two fugitives had perished in the wind of the wilderness. You swore that your people and your hounds had hunted for them throughout the black land and the red desert surrounding the city. You came to me, and you told me that they could not have escaped nor found shelter and, therefore, must have surrendered to the sands of the desert. But look.

They have fooled you and chosen to dwell for many days in the tomb near the temple, which they so shamefully desecrated. And when it was time for them to leave their hiding, they did so and slew one of your warriors. The whitehaired one must have done this, for there is no trace of him. Nor is there any sign of the horse, which means, Haugha, that he has taken one of your own beasts. And the other, the slave of the temple, he too would have fled if not for the wrath of god, who crushed the life out of him before he could leave the tomb. But you see that his death is no service of yours. Therefore, where is your answer, for you have deceived me greatly and permitted the profaner of the Living Effigy of Sebek, the god to pass through this land on one of your own horses."

But the chief guard lowered his head and remained silent.

"Speak!" said Het-Ka-Sebek. His voice was calm. "Speak while I reflect upon the kind of death you will die."

"Master, I know not how to reply. It was never my intention to deceive you, for I myself truly believed what I saw and what I uttered. My life, as always, is in your hands."

But now it was Het-Ka-Sebek who remained silent. He closed his eyes. And when he opened them, the dark-skinned warrior was still kneeling motionless by his feet, with his head in the dust and his hands outstretched, as if he was expecting a sudden blow.

"As you know, there are many vast ant-hills in the groves around the lake," spoke the priest quietly. "Some of them flourish beneath the great sycamore trees. And all of them are like cities of eternal hunger. If you were tied high up in the branches with cuts in your skin, the smell of blood would entice those small and busy creatures into working their way up to you in an endless line. And each one of them would return to their city with a tiny piece of your flesh. You could live on for a day, perhaps several days, for they usually feast upon the lower half of the body first. And it is known that such men remain in agony, even after their legs have been eaten to the bone. Have you ever seen such an execution?"

But the kneeling one remained silent and motionless.

"But I," continued Het-Ka-Sebek calmly, "am patient, too patient. The boy has fled. But he is still alive, for only the living slay those who live themselves and then escape with their horses. Therefore he must be somewhere, a long way away, for this time, he is much further than when you last lost track of him. And so listen to me, you, who are still chief of the desert guards. Find him and bring him back alive, and if you do, I shall forget what you have done, and your name will remain among the living. But if you fail to find him, I shall surrender you to the ants, and they will teach you your duties. For neither you, Haugha, nor your warriors, nor indeed any of your hounds had found that defenseless mortal, but be you sure that the ants will waste no time in finding you, even amongst the highest of branches. Therefore assemble your men at once and remember, you have but one task and all others must be forsaken until you seek out and bring before me that whitehaired boy."

"Master!" whispered the chief and kissed his golden sandals, but Het-Ka-Sebek would have none of this and gently pushed him aside with his foot.

"Away with you! I have no wish to hear your voice."

He turned back and approached his litter.

There was a place where the great river flowed in a much narrower channel, between the towering rugged rocks of a ravine it had cut through a chain of low mountains, and it was here that the city of Sem-Her could be found. Many centuries ago, it had started out as a small fishing village, for the waters of the sacred river rose and fell here without ever depositing any of its blessed silt and thus sentenced the area to everlasting infertility. But with the passage of time, the city grew in importance, becoming a place where goods traveling from Upper Egypt down to the Delta were reloaded. On one side, the sands of the desert rolled to the west, and on the other, the rugged mountains stretched as far as the sea, where, in the distant South lay the Land of Punt.

The city of Sem-Her occupied both banks of the river, and

together with its temples and the palace of the governor of his holiness, the Pharaoh, it was a solitary island of green, situated in a lifeless wilderness burning in the sun. Only from the roof of the temples and through a bluish haze was it possible to catch a glimpse of the distant verdure along the river. But here, the world was dead and hostile to man. Reeds never grew beside the fast-flowing, turgid river, and crocodiles were rare visitors, for the impetuous current pushing between the rocky banks showed friendship to no one.

"Your brothers, guardians of the temple of Sebek by the Great Lake, send greetings to you, O most venerable one. And with these greetings, they send this here scroll so that your most pious eyes may deign to look upon it and decide if you choose to act as the many centuries of true friendship between your temple and ours no doubt shall prompt you to," said the young priest in a quiet monotone.

He stood before an aged man sitting upon a gilt throne and wearing nothing but a gold loincloth and equally gold sandals, which he rested upon a footstool made in the shape of a fleshy, kneeling hippopotamus with a wide and bulging back.

"Read it," said the aged man softly.

"Yes, O most venerable one!"

The young priest unfurled the scroll and started reading, passing it between his fingers.

"The servants of the temple of Sebek send greetings to the high priest of Ptah, the god, and father of almighty gods..."

He fell silent for a while and lowered his head before continuing:

"The news of the most foul sacrilege perpetrated in the holy city of Sekhem has long reached your ears. We thought, in our ignorance, that the gods themselves had punished the guilty by burying them beneath the sands of the wilderness during a storm. But now we have proof that this has not happened and that only one of the guilty has perished, while the other has escaped and is likely heading north to avoid punishment. There is but one way for him. He must slip past the city of Sem-Her in a boat, at night. But you, O most high servant of the powerful Ptah, have the power to prevent it, for only one word is needed, and your warriors will appear along the river, and their keen eyes and weapons will be enough to seize him. He will find no shelter in the wilderness surrounding the city that defies the presence of both grove and thicket or any reeds that flourish along the river banks in other parts of its watercourse. We ask you in the name of our friendship and the respect we have for you and for your god, which, together with the priests of the high temple you serve, to apprehend and return the seized malefactor alive under the strictest guard to the house of Sebek by the Great Lake."

The priest rolled up the papyrus.

"The most venerable Het-Ka-Sebek has ordered me to add that our gratitude to the servants of the great Ptah will be expressed before his feast-day, when he himself will arrive with our brothers, with our thanks to you, O most venerable one, for showing your great power and kindness by seizing the murderer. And he wishes to add that the one he seeks is a young boy with very white hair and skin extremely pale, the kind of which has never been seen before by the people of this country."

The aged man remained silent. At last he nodded, stretched forth his hand, and took hold of a small silver rod with which he struck a bronze gong.

Two priests entered and stood waiting by the door.

"Let the guards of the river and port be doubled. Should a solitary figure appear circling round the city or attempting to pass it along the river, he must be seized, but it is forbidden to harm him in any way. His hair is of white color, and his skin is pale. This is a matter of absolute importance, and it is the brothers of the Great Lake who have asked us for our help."

CHAPTER TEN
And He Was Swallowed By Darkness

At midday, when the sun stood at the zenith, pouring down its heat so that everything fell silent, a large green bird with a long red bill settled next to a boat hidden in the dense sea of tall reeds.

Whitehair slowly reached for his bow. Only a tiny stretch of water and a few reeds leaning in the direction of the lazy current separated him from the bird. It was observing him. And at any time, it could fly away, but it remained in its place, knowing that the creature before its eyes was too far to harm it in any way, and should the creature move too suddenly or try to approach, the bird would seek the air for protection.

The arrow whistled softly, and the bird fell into the water lifeless. The young Trojan dipped his oar softly and, without a splash, approached the bird.

Quickly he pulled the arrow out and washed it. He then plucked the bird and ripped it apart with his dagger, throwing away its entrails. Afterward he severed its head and neck and sank his teeth in the still-warm flesh, tearing pieces of it away and devouring them.

He threw the bones away and, resuming his rowing without disturbing the water, crept along, propelled by the north-bound current. A great plain of turbid water stretched to his right, but where Whitehair was, everything was calm, and only a barely detectable current pushed its way through the reeds, indicating the flow of the river. Three days had passed since he had first glimpsed the vast waters, bathing in the pale radiance of daybreak.

He recalled how he had jumped off his horse and slapped its side mightily to drive the frightened beast away and how it ran away into the wilderness at a trot, and how he had walked on foot to the river. At that hour, the villagers were still asleep, so he was able to find a small boat easily, and when he looked inside, he was filled with joy, for it contained a strong oar and two water skins. But he did not paddle out too far, for he wished to hide among the reeds and creep slowly northwards, winding his way through the rushes and water thickets. They were so high that he could stand straight up in his boat and still remain hidden from view.

For the whole next day and night, he stole along without the slightest rest and then again for the whole of the following day until he finally pulled into deep thickets, and there, a heavy sleep descended upon him. And in all this time, not once did he see a living creature, apart from the two solitary crocodiles which appeared when his boat floated onto an open stretch of water surrounded by reeds, but even they withdrew quickly and plunged into the depths.

It was dark when he woke, so he used the cloak of night to continue north, believing that nourishment would come by itself, for already he had eaten all the onions and was growing weak. And though much life lurked in the reeds, the greenish bird with the long bill was his first meal. But he paddled carefully now, and slower than ever, for the reeds were thinning out, and frequently the boat floated onto tiny areas of open water which glinted before his eyes.

Suddenly he stopped in front of a cluster of papyrus and looked at their stems. They resembled the outstretched palms of humans and leaned against each other, creating a tunnel above the water.

Lying flat at the bottom of the boat, he lifted his head a little and, rowing noiselessly with his hands, moved along almost imperceptibly, like a log floating upon the idle current.

Gradually, the reeds grew thinner until eventually they grew only in clusters, and, as he looked into the distance, a chain of red hills loomed out for the first time, followed by a remote city that appeared upon the towering banks of the river. The river before him grew narrower, splitting up into a number of channels where it was beaten into a yellow froth as it gushed among tremendous boulders. Now, the reflections of sunlight on the water yielded to a quick, tall wave that rolled in front of him.

Rowing backward, he reentered a thick cluster of tall reeds, and, remaining hidden deep inside, looked out at the scenery stretching before his eyes.

He waited. And shortly afterward, a small ship came into view. There was something strange about its movement, for it traveled neither south nor north, as most ships its size did, but instead, having approached from the city, it moved neither upstream nor downstream but wandered from one bank to the other, tacking its sail from left to right, and in turn dipping its oars on either side. It appeared to be awaiting someone. Whitehair turned his eyes towards the hills. They were bleak, deprived of vegetation, and forbidding. On top of one of the nearest hills, he saw two men. They were standing motionless, leaning upon their long spears.

"The one I slew has been found," was a thought that had tormented his mind for the past three days. "They have found him and realized at once that we are still alive. But poor Lauratas rests in the tomb, and they are not aware of this, so they think there are two of us. They must think we had hidden in the mountains surrounding the Valley of the Dead and that we have chosen to move only now. And since the river is the only way of escape, surely they are waiting for us here. I struck their god. I slew him. They will not rest until they find me."

Instinctively, he lifted his hand out of the water, for a crocodile could easily swim up noiselessly, seize him and pull him into the turbid, yellowish current, thus avenging Sebek. He kept on observing. The ship continued to tack about upon the river while the people on the hills trotted there and back as if they were taking a stroll. They could not be herdsmen, for they had no animals with them, and moreover, no beast could find pasture in this sun-scorched wilderness. The sun was gradually dipping down towards the horizon, but the great heat persisted. Whitehair cupped his hands, scooped out some water, and started drinking.

Hidden in the shadow of bulrushes, he observed what went on. A huge fish splashed out of the muddy current and plunged back into the depths. The heavens above were cloudless, and only a few red birds glided upon their motionless, outstretched wings. They flew past the ship and, getting lower and lower, faded in the distance.

It was where the river grew narrower and where its waters rushed with greater speed that the vessel was waiting. A little further on, near the city, the white sails of many boats could be seen. Undoubtedly fishermen or boatmen were busying themselves there.

If the ship remained upon the water and did not return to the city before dark, he would have no chance of sneaking past them because the night on the open water would offer him no cover at all. Even the darkest of nights would not be dark enough, for the twinkle of stars would reveal his boat to the sharp eyes of the guards. And could he even hope to keep to the very edge, having only a single oar and his own strength to fight the tempestuous, rumbling, and overflowing current?

"What if I go back and abandon my boat and then, using the cloak of night, try to pass the mountains and that city on foot?"

He thought for a while and quickly realized that he had no other choice. He had to move north in the direction of the sea beyond which lay his native city, Troy of Kings. But if Het-Ka-Sebek had foreseen his intentions, would he not have obstructed the way along the river and ordered his warriors to keep vigil in the mountains? Moreover, would not his desert guards be riding their swift horses right now and searching the sands of either bank in the company of their hounds? The Great Lake was a long way from here, but the power of the temple of Sebek was surely mighty enough to reach him here. He knew nothing of the customs of this land, but word of his flight must have spread far and wide, much further than he had traveled, for he believed that these people had a great understanding for one another.

He sighed. If he turned back now, he would be retreating from the sea, but there was nothing else he could do. Remaining in the safety of the reeds, he turned his boat round and, dipping his oars in the water, turned back into the dense sea of reeds.

When night came, he dipped one of his water skins into the river, then the other one, and waited patiently as they filled while bubbles of air floated to the surface, each one carrying a tiny sparkle of silver—a gift of the light shining down from the thin crescent of the moon.

Then tying the skins with a strap, he threw them over his shoulder. With his bow upon his other shoulder and a dagger in his hand, he jumped onto the miry bank.

At first, he found himself surrounded by tall reeds. He crept along cautiously, trying to see through the darkness, fearing not only men but also beasts. At last, he reached the end of the reeds. Before him, a hill steadily ascended into the sky. It was completely devoid of any vegetation, dry and still hot with the heat of the day. Before he started climbing it, he looked into the distance, where the gloomy sky melted into the gloomy land, and searched for anything that moved. He crept away from the reeds and, crouching down, started climbing towards the top of the hill, hiding behind boulders covering the hillside. When he finally crawled onto the summit, he clung to the ground and looked about.

Behind him, among the sea of reeds, the broad silver river slithered along like a great snake moving slowly towards the northern horizon, and before him, a limitless chain of hills, bathed in soft moonlight, stretching on into the distance. It was to his right, where the river could be seen no longer, that the city he had seen by day had to be situated. And if he wanted to pass it, it would mean a long trek around it through the hills.

He looked into the sky, for he wished to remember the constellations. One of the first things he had ever learned was that only one star remained in its place throughout the night and that this was the star which guided fishermen back to their native shores. He found it again and once more looked at the hills. Then, stopping to grip his dagger, he began to descend.

For the whole of the night, he walked on and on, and only when daybreak produced a faint glow in the east did the young Trojan search out a hollow amongst the rocks and lie down in it. The night had been cold, but with the coming of the day, a feeling of warmth embraced his body. Curled up and drowned in the deep shadow of boulders, the fugitive fell asleep.

Many times he woke from his dreams, dreams which spoke now of his childhood days and now of recent events, and his memory was like a piece of earthenware, beautifully painted but shattered beyond all hope of repair, behind his closed eyelids. But each time, he would fall asleep again, and when he had rested enough, he opened his eyes and saw that the sun had wandered across the heavens as far as the red hills upon the horizon.

The river was such a long way behind him that even the valley in which it flowed could not be seen. Only the rolling sands of the wilderness and bleak rocky ridges surrounded him now. Still lying down, he looked at the dunes which stretched away into the horizon. Nothing enlivened the scene of desolation. No living creature, nor tree, nor even a blade of grass. He sat up straight, took hold of a water skin, and drank what was left inside, but the water was so warm and foul that he could barely swallow it.

Dusk was falling. Whitehair considered digging a hole in the ground to bury the empty water skin, but, reconsidering, he slung it over his shoulder, together with the other one, which was still full. He inspected his bow carefully and, plucking its string to test it, moved on.

The stars began to twinkle in the sky, and one glance at them told him that he was moving in the right direction. If only the river would flow along a more accessible and less rocky bed! He had eaten all of his food and had left his boat behind, but he believed that after circling around the city and returning to the river, he would find both craft and nourishment again.

He would walk north for half the night and then turn and walk towards the river almost perpendicularly, looking for shelter along its banks. Without water, he could not hope to wander in the wilderness much longer than that.

He walked along vigilantly, keeping away from the hillsides and ridges soaked in moonlight, from which one could look into the distance but also upon which the dark figure of a mortal could easily be seen.

Before midnight he turned towards the river expecting to reach it by dawn, providing it did not turn east beyond the city. He entered a deep and rocky ravine. It was full of boulders, which had once been part of the hillside. Absolute silence filled the air. Picking his way among the debris, he neither noticed nor heard the two black shapes which emerged from among the rocks and, stealthily creeping along, pounced upon him from behind.

And only when a heavy piece of canvas wrapped around his body and two pairs of powerful hands gripped him did he realize that nothing could save him. He struggled on violently and tried to grasp his dagger, which dangled upon his neck, but it was all in vain, for his assailants tore his hands from under the canvas and, wasting no time, bound them behind his back.

Once again, in desperation, he attempted to free himself, but at the same time, someone hit him mightily on the back of the head, and his mind was rendered insensible.

When he woke, he found himself lying on dry, cold sand. He was filled with dread and uncertainty, for at first, he remembered nothing of what had passed and tried to sit up. At once, he fell back again, gritting his teeth and suppressing a groan, for a violent pain stung the back of his head. He moved his hands. The bonds were gone. He touched the sheath upon his chest, but his dagger was there no longer. He heard someone speaking in the distance, and only now did he recall what had happened.

Still lying down and not daring to move his head, he looked about.

Close by, a small group of people flocked together: five men and two women. They were all Egyptian peasants, for they were wearing short robes of plain cloth, and each one had his hair cropped like the slaves of the great temple and the peasants who labored in the fields around the lake. They sat in a compact circle, and their heads were drooping, like the heads of those whose fates have been blackened with ill fortune. One of the men had a long and bloody gash upon his face, and Whitehair could see that he had been smitten recently with a mighty blow, for his face was still swollen badly.

A little further along, an armed warrior sat upon the sand with his legs crossed, and in his hand, he held a short spear. His face was utterly savage, and his long black hair ran down in curls over a large copper ring in his ear. He was half-naked. Some distance behind him, a camp had been set up. Several horses could be seen there, and a small group of warriors occupied themselves by shooting a bow at an invisible target. Whitehair screwed up his eyes and recognized his own weapon.

One of the women broke the silence whispering something to her companion, who breathed back an answer. The guard looked up and shouted at them. Whitehair understood nothing, but he knew at once that they had been forbidden to speak. The woman nestled her head against her shoulder and pressed it down even lower. And silence fell again.

And so they had hunted him down. But if these were the desert guards, why were they not tearing along to Het-Ka-Sebek, who must be eager to hear news of him? Maybe their horses were too wearied after the pursuit and must rest before their trek across the wilderness? But who were these people next to him, for they too had been pounced upon and made prisoners? He felt a dryness in his throat, and reaching for his water skin lying nearby, uncorked it and started to drink. The others observed him indifferently.

One of the warriors occupying himself with the bow shouted something in their direction, and their guard stood up and shouted back, brandishing his spear. All the prisoners jumped up at once. Whitehair stood up also. He touched the back of his head, and when he saw his palm, a great relief filled his heart, for there was no blood upon it. Till now, he had been convinced he had an open wound, but apparently, he had been struck with a blunt tool to knock him senseless. No doubt the hunters were under strict orders from Het-Ka-Sebek not to harm him. No doubt he wanted to get the young Trojan alive, and only afterward would he...

He shuddered.

Two warriors approached and herded the captives uphill towards the horses, prodding them with the shafts of their spears. Several men were saddling the animals already, placing bundles and water skins on their backs. A figure riding a black horse slowly descended from one of the nearby dunes and urged everyone to hurry by shouting at them harshly. It was clear that he was the leader, and at his signal, the Egyptians scrambled onto the pack horses, ten in all, all of which were tied together by ropes. One of the guards mounted the first and another one the last so that the prisoners remained in the middle. The rest rode on in front. But Whitehair remained where he was, undecided.

"If I start running into the wilderness," he thought, "maybe one of them will pierce me with his spear. And thus, I shall avoid the pool in which Sebek dwells!"

He hesitated for a while and then recalled that he had already once managed an escape and that while he was still alive, it was impossible to foresee the end, for even Lauratas agreed that matters such as these were in the hands of the gods alone who held in derision both mortal pride and despair.

He staggered forward, for the pain in the back of his head still persisted, and approached one of the horses, clambered on, and grasped the dark mane with both hands.

A sharp order resounded, and the animals began to move.

The sun had already risen, but the heat of the day grew rapidly. Whitehair heaved a sigh. A sudden hunger gripped him. But he knew he would receive no nourishment. He pressed his lips together and closed his eyes, permitting the sun to caress the right-hand side of his face with warmth.

And then he shuddered. Something strange was happening, something he failed to understand. His aching head made him struggle to arrange his thoughts, which only wandered about, refusing to give a clear picture of the events which were taking place.

And so he rode on, filled with a knowledge that something unknown, something beyond credibility, was occurring. He could feel his mind unraveling a great mystery and telling him all, but still, he was unable to grasp the meaning.

And then, suddenly, he realized it! The horses were heading north! Not south, towards the tall priest, who held in his hand a golden staff bearing the likeness of Sebek, and who awaited his arrival in the temple by the Great Lake.

For a long while, he sat upon his beast, jogged from side to side, as its swift legs covered the ground at a trot, and he tried to understand why this was happening.

There could be but one answer: these were not the servants of Het-Ka-Sebek, nor indeed the guards of the desert.

But who could they be?

One of the riders at the front broke away and slowly trotted back. As soon as he reached Whitehair, he turned his horse around and approached his side.

The young Trojan lifted his head. And now the rider spoke in a sharp, guttural voice, clearly addressing him.

Whitehair spread his arms and answered:

"I know not what you say, warrior."

The other man listened, flashed his eyes, and raised his arm as if making ready to strike him, but clearly changed his mind, for he shouted out aloud towards the others. Another rider broke away from the front. They exchanged a few quick words.

"Do you belong to the People of the Sea?" said the second man. He broke and maimed the tongue with which the people of the islands spoke but was clear enough for Whitehair to understand.

"Yes, master. I am a Trojan, the son of a fisherman."

"A Trojan?" clearly, the man was baffled by these words. "Are you from the People of the Sea, I ask?"

"Yes, master."

The warriors spoke to one another.

"How is it that you are in this land? And who gave you such a beautiful bow and these rich ornaments of gold? Your father must be a king and will pay well to see you again?"

"My father is no king. And the ornaments and bow I took from the tomb of a wealthy man in this land."

Whitehair spoke slowly because he wished the listening man to grasp the meaning of his every word. But also, it was his intention to gain time, for his mind was still confused. He must speak the truth as much as possible, keeping only the worst to himself. And never could he allow them to learn that the priest of the great temple sought him, for they would hand him over at once, demanding a high ransom, and they would surely get it. These people were the nomads of the desert who attacked the border villages to take slaves and sold them to the highest bidder.

"How have you come to be here?"

"I was fishing when a great storm arose and cast me onto the open waters. A certain wealthy merchant who was sailing to this land saw me upon the sea. He sold me to a certain master of this land, but I escaped from him, wanting to return to my own people. During my flight, you seized me and made me your captive."

Again the two riders spoke amongst themselves.

"Have you spoken the truth? Is your father not a man of wealth?"

"If he were, would not I say so at once so that he would pay you and take me back to my native home?"

They appeared to be convinced by his words and spurred

their beasts on without even glancing back at him.

Whitehair drank a little water and, dripping the remaining drops onto his hand, dried it with his tongue. Gradually the sun floated higher and higher, and now the heat was almost unbearable. He raised the empty water skin overhead, trying to shield himself from the merciless rays.

The horses trotted on steadily, climbing one dune, descending it, and then climbing another. An endless world of burning sands unfolded before their eyes, totally empty and utterly dreadful and never capable of supporting a living creature.

And though Whitehair knew the truth now—that these cruel warriors of the desert had made him prisoner and that only one fate awaited him, the fate of a slave, he felt no fear or gloom in his heart. Not only he but his captors also must fear meeting their eternal foes, the guards of the desert. The only allies he could have met in this land were precisely these savages while he struggled desperately for survival in the middle of a strange land, a land which did nothing but hunt him.

What really mattered was that they were constantly heading north, and each step the horses took was one step closer to the sea.

On the fourth day of their journey, they turned northeast, and on the tenth, just as the sun rose, Whitehair peered into the distance, as far as the furthest sand dunes, and saw a plain, which appeared to be dark and almost black in color. But as the sun rose higher and the plain even closer, it changed its appearance and became dark blue. The young Trojan touched his forehead with his fist, stretching out his other hand in a greeting. But nobody spared him even a glance.

The sun had already journeyed over half the heavens when they approached a village situated away from the sea, close to a freshwater spring, surrounded by a ring of palm trees and a meadow upon which many horses pastured. At once, they were given water and nourishment, and Whitehair was now certain that they were destined for sale, for otherwise, why feed them? In fact, not once during their journey had they been beaten or otherwise abused. Their guards had treated them with the same indifference with which they treated their pack horses. They were just like animals fattened for slaughter.

Before dusk, an old man approached the enclosure where they had been placed, inspected them, and walked away. No doubt, he was the chieftain. Later on, they were driven into another enclosure on the other side of the village, where other prisoners were already gathered, and together they spent the night, accompanied only by the twinkling of the stars.

A few days passed uneventfully. At last, on a certain morning, a warrior appeared and beckoned Whitehair. It was the man who spoke his tongue.

"Follow me!" he ordered him.

And now they walked up to some clay huts, crowded together near the freshwater spring.

They entered one of them, and at first, the young Trojan could not see anything because it was so dark.

"Kneel!" shouted the warrior from behind. But before Whitehair could do so he felt an iron grip upon his shoulder and was thrown to the ground near the feet of the old man whom he had first seen on the evening of his arrival.

The old man uttered a few words which Whitehair did not follow, and the warrior bowed. He gripped the Trojan's shoulder again and lifted him onto his feet.

With his eyes more accustomed to the dark, Whitehair saw a low and flat slab of stone which probably served as a table. His weapons and other belongings were lying upon it.

"Yohuga, the master of your life, asks you if you spoke the truth when you claimed to be the son of a fisherman from a distant land?"

"Yes, master. I am the son of a fisherman."

The old man looked at the Trojan with probing eyes.

Presently he uttered a few words in the tongue of the People of the Sea and spoke them with greater ease than the one who had served as his interpreter.

"Tell me, which tomb did you enter? And moreover, how did you manage to do it?"

"I ran away from my owner with a companion, and our path took us through the City of the Dead, which was near the city of the living in which I had been held. Then we met the great wind of the wilderness. But just at that time, we happened to come upon an unsealed tomb and took refuge in it. After the storm subsided and before we left the tomb to continue our flight, we took some of the objects which would serve us on our way."

"Where is your companion?"

"He perished beneath a huge rock."

Silence fell.

"Do many objects, such as these ornaments of gold, remain within that tomb?"

"Yes, master. And also many beautiful weapons and all kinds of other riches."

"Tell me, could you return to this valley and seek the tomb out yet again?"

"No, master, for I recall but one thing about the Valley of the Dead. It is near the city to which I had been taken. But we had sailed for many days from the seashore south, on the great river before we reached that city. After I escaped, I first crept north along the river banks for many days. But later, I ran into the wilderness for fear of meeting people near a city on the river. And then I was seized by your warriors."

The old man remained silent and brushed his fingers over the bow in front of him. A dagger rested among the objects on the slab of stone, which Whitehair recognized as his own. And now the old man stretched his hand towards it.

"Why is it that this dagger of such little value is among all these things when this other one is such a fine piece of work?"

"This one, master, was with me when I was fished out of the sea. But the precious one I took from the tomb, of which I have already spoken."

The old man shook his head.

"Maybe your words are full of truth? And yet they could be a creation of your mind, though you are young. I have traded with people who speak your tongue for many years. They are crafty merchants and full of cunning and prepared to kill whenever they see it as a bargain. Moreover, they care nothing for words nor indeed for oaths, even when they call upon their gods as witnesses. Therefore, I believe that a good flogging could refresh your memory concerning the location of this tomb. But my warriors are wearied. They have traveled far and wide, seeking prisoners for sale to the islands. Maybe you have spoken the truth, but again, you could have nourished us with lies. Soon the merchant pirates who speak your tongue will arrive in their speedy ships. You are young and healthy, and they will gladly buy you. There is a silver mine in a distant land which needs many slaves. Those who enter it are doomed, for it is a place of no return."

And he fell silent for a while.

"Leave now. If you have spoken the truth, the merchants will have you. But if you are hiding something which could bring us great profit, lead my people to the tomb where riches such as these can be found," he placed his hand upon the table. "Then you might be spared if their value greatly exceeds your own. Leave now and see if your memory revives."

He waved his hand to the warrior and pointed at the objects before him. Quickly they were wrapped in a linen cloth and placed in the corner of the room.

When the young Trojan returned to the enclosure where the captives were held, he sat down upon the grass and started considering what the old man had said. It would take a journey of many days to reach the temple and the pool, which by now was surely inhabited by another Sebek, as ferocious as the one he had slain but perhaps younger and stronger and less spoiled. It would not be wise to go anywhere near that place. His second option—to remember nothing and be sold to the People of the Sea—seemed by far the better one. For even if the silver mines were as bad as the old man said, he would never meet the fate of that white goat.

He shuddered and lifted his head. Three horseriders were approaching from the wilderness. One of them had his hands tied behind his back whilst the remaining two trotted along on either side, each one armed with a short spear and a bow. The one in the middle sat straight and was looking about curiously. They disappeared behind the trees, heading for the huts.

Whitehair picked a blade of grass and breathed in deeply. He had made his decision. Not a word would he utter to these people about the tomb of Nerau-Ta, the scribe. How could they get there anyway, and roll that huge boulder away which had crushed his friend, Lauratas?

Once more, he shuddered and stretched back upon the grass and looked into the heavens with unseeing eyes, for his thoughts were upon his native land, and he wondered who would purchase him from the People of the Wilderness and where the silent black ships of the merchants of the sea would take him.

CHAPTER ELEVEN
The Hands of Priests Stretch to the Ends of the Earth

The three horsemen whom Whitehair had seen descending from the hill arrived before the hut of the old chieftain. One of them dismounted and walked inside.

"Master..." he said, bowing his head before the old man who sat still behind the stone table. "We have captured a certain man."

The chieftain replaced the mug of water from which he was about to drink.

"Speak!"

"He is one of the desert guards."

The old man became motionless.

"He has ventured a long way," his voice was nearly inaudible. "Was he alone?"

"Yes, master. We were patrolling the wilderness some distance from the village, a journey of half a day, when he emerged from out of the hills and started to approach us. And when he came nearer, he took hold of his weapons and cast them upon the ground. Then he spoke unto us, expressing his wish to see the master of this land and claiming to have tidings for him. We would have slain him, master, but it came to our minds that we can only do this at your command after we bring him before your presence, and moreover, we thought you might wish to learn what kind of mission brings him here."

"You have done well. Bring him in."

The warrior slipped out and presently returned with his

companion and the captive, who fell onto his knees at once, touched the ground before the old man with his head, stood up, and began to speak.

"Valiant Haugha, chief of the warriors who guard the Great Lake, which lies deep inside the land of our divine Pharaoh—may he live forever!—sends greetings to you, even though you realize that you and others of the wilderness, like yourselves, will never cease to be his enemies."

"That is true," said the old chieftain pleasantly. "We are his enemies and also the enemies of the pharaoh he serves. But for sure, he is the greater enemy of the two, for it is the dog and not the master which bites and which we despise the most. What made him send you here? Was it to seek out certain death at the hands of my warriors? Does he know not that anyone who passes out of the land of Egypt is as good as lost?"

"He knows all this, O chieftain, and I, his messenger, know this also, and so do our other warriors, whom he has sent out to many other chieftains of the tribes in the wilderness who constantly violate the boundaries of Egypt. But he has decided that our lives are of little importance compared to the gravity of the business on which he sends us. We had no choice but to obey."

"If your chief, Haugha, serves the Great Lake, it means he also serves the temple of the crocodile. Is this not so?"

"Yes, master."

"Does Haugha, your chief, for reasons still unknown to me, wish to become a free man, to seize many prisoners, cross into the desert, and become a member of our tribe, and never again be a dog in the service of the priests, who so unthinkingly worship a mere animal? Does he want to become a free lion which prowls the desert wherever it wishes and pounces upon any prey it wishes to take, which is what we, the People of the Wilderness, do?"

"No, master. Though he might have done so, for he is threatened with a most pitiless death. But we have served the temple from time immemorial and its land has become our land. Moreover, we have our wives and children there, and therefore we cannot turn traitor, for then our families would suffer terribly at the hands of the priests. And it would be almost impossible for the whole tribe to escape, for with women and children, we would move slowly, and an army would be sent in pursuit of us, and not only our families, but we ourselves would be struck down."

"Speak of the danger which faces your master."

"He ordered me not to speak a word of this, but I shall reveal the whole truth because I stand before my enemies who may thrust a spear into my heart whenever it is their wish to do so. A sacrilege has been perpetrated in our temple. Our god, the crocodile, the one you so greatly despise, has been slain. A boy who was to be his offering did this. He fled, and we have been unable to seize him, even though our land is strange to his eyes, for he belongs to the People of the Sea and is so unlike Egyptians that anyone can recognize him with ease."

"Describe the one you speak of," said the old man without concern.

"His hair is white, as white as that of an egret, and his skin is no darker than the plumes of the *goala* bird. Even among the People of the Sea, such hair has never been seen."

"Tell me more. You say he slew the beast you worship, and you, the desert guards, have not been able to catch him?"

"This is not all. He fled the temple with another slave, a man who had been a slave at the temple for fully twenty years, and the two had found their way into a sealed tomb and hidden there for twenty days. Afterward, he killed one of our men, stole his horse, and fled again. And now the blame has fallen on my valiant master, Haugha, who will be devoured by ants if we fail to seek out and return the fugitive to the temple. But neither we nor the river guards can say where he is. But we came across footprints in the wilderness and guessed that someone must have seized him, for an arrow belonging to the tomb where he had sheltered lay upon the ground, and there were traces of a struggle and further on a place where horses had been hidden, which later rode away. But we had arrived much too late, for otherwise, the valiant Haugha would have caught your warriors and infallibly struck them down, snatching the prisoner away. We also know that a number of people were seized from the adjoining villages by the river. The whole group left a trail leading towards the north, then northeast, but our trackers turned back, for without water they could go on no longer."

He sighed and spread his arms.

"The valiant Haugha does not deny that his warriors could never hope to cross the desert unobserved and descend upon you by surprise, for you know the desert as well as we do, and you have many watchful scouts everywhere. And, forewarned by your scouts of our attack, you would call on other desert tribes to come to your defense, and then we could never hope to defeat you. Besides, as uncertain as such a plan of action would be, it may all be in vain in any case, for not knowing his value to our temple, you may already have sold the boy with white hair or slain him. My master, the valiant Haugha, refuses to resort to lies and tricks and wishes to treat you with the respect you deserve, even though you are his enemy. Therefore, he sends me here to utter words of truth. If the fugitive is alive and in your hands, you will receive twenty other young and healthy men in exchange for him, which my master, Haugha, will seize and bring before you, in such a way that the whole exchange remains a secret forever, so that you may feel free to do with them as you please. And if you desire not people, who are your principal trading good, but something else, then speak, and my valiant master will do everything in his power to satisfy your requirements."

The old man remained silent for some time.

"If the one he seeks were here," spoke he quietly, "I would surely sell him to your temple. Knowing what riches the priests possess, I rest assured that they would reward me more generously for the perpetrator of a sacrilege than your master, Haugha, who is nowhere near as wealthy or powerful. What good would it serve me to make a trade with Haugha, your master? Let the ants devour him. He is a foolish chief and moreover, a miserable guard if a mere boy in a strange land and completely on his own can evade him. If I ordered this warrior behind you to pierce your back with his spear, it would be most fitting. Then, I should waste no time in sending messengers to your temple, for no one would harm them, even though Egypt is our enemy. Why, they would be received politely, welcomed with food and drink, and entertained and given many precious goods. And the priests would offer many gifts for the boy, for in their utter stupidity they nourish crocodiles with men, when in fact they should slay all these creatures until not one was left."

The messenger looked down in silence.

"And yet," continued the old man, "this chief of yours can reward us better than the temple. My warriors must travel south, circling around the lake in order to reach the land where so many people dwell. They are excellent merchandise and are gladly purchased by the merchants of the islands. But the guards of the wilderness have denied us entry into that land for a long time now, thus forcing us to forsake our expeditions south. Go in peace and tell your master that the one he seeks will return to him alive and well if your eyes remain closed to us for no less than three months. A multitude of warriors belonging to many tribes of my people will then gather together and venture into the land to the south, returning with spoils, bringing a vast number of slaves, and then... then your boy will be returned to your master. But if your valiant master, Haugha, is willing to come before me and swear to agree to these conditions and to honor them, he will receive the boy at once. And then we shall hold him, your master, until our expedition has ended, but the priests will have their fugitive almost at once."

"But master, the temple would never tolerate such a thing, nor indeed would the governor of our god-like Pharaoh."

"The armies of Egypt have no other eyes in the western wilderness but yours. After my people have passed the lake, unnoticed by your guards—who will, of course, be busy looking for my men elsewhere—my men and their spoils will melt into the sands so that no one will know of their crossing. For they are like the wind and the spirits of the dead, and there is no reason why the priests of your temple, or the ruler of Egypt should ever hear of this."

"I shall repeat your words, master, in every detail."

"I shall wait for an answer till the next full moon. Seven nights have passed since it was last full. Therefore you have enough time ahead of you. But if on that day we have not seen your master, Haugha, here, a messenger of mine will ride forth and inform the priests of the crocodile that we have him, whom they seek, and then your valiant Haugha will be devoured by those tiny, though valiant ants. Away with you!"

Then turning to his warriors, he said:

"Let him ride through the wilderness a free man, but first take him to see the boy with white hair and let his eyes feed upon the sight of him so that he may return and report to his master what he had seen and heard. Then supply him with nourishment and water, lest he should drop of exhaustion, and give him two companions for his journey to make sure that he reaches his master safely."

The warrior prostrated himself and left the abode.

Having drunk some of the water, the old man rose and walked to the corner. There he unwrapped the piece of cloth with his bare foot and touched the gold earrings with his toes. He bent down, lifted the dagger belonging to Whitehair, and smiled.

"No doubt he slew the beast with this dagger," he murmured to himself. "A truly brave warrior, and yet so young. May the gods have mercy and give him a fast death when the wrath of the crocodile temple descends upon him."

He turned around and, approaching the entrance, pulled back the curtain of horse leather. The sun was shining overhead. It was almost noon.

The old man looked at the contours of the dunes, and again a smile appeared upon his lips. The thought of the great expedition which would bring many slaves from the southern land gladdened him. Passage by the lake, under the watchful eyes of the desert guards, had been until now impossible. At times a few riders would manage to slip past and return with a handful of slaves. But any larger expedition was doomed to fail, for the guards would waste no time in notifying the Pharaoh, whose armies would then prevent their return from the south and strike each one of them down. And now there was a way to make those eternally wakeful eyes heavy and sleepy, and when this happened, he would form an alliance with the chieftains of other villages, and with one great effort, they would strike. Such an expedition could bring thousands upon thousands of slaves, young, healthy men, and women, for which they would demand salt, iron, gold, and many, many other riches which the sands of the wilderness, his home and place of birth, could never produce.

Seven days later, one of the guards standing watch upon a nearby hill came running down towards the village, calling out that two ships had approached the shore. They had stopped some distance offshore and were waiting with lowered sails.

They waited for a long time until, at last, the chieftains of the village appeared with a group of warriors upon the shore. Then one of the ships approached to within a shouting distance. A man at the prow, clad in a cuirass of bronze, a tall helm with a red panache, and with a brightly painted shield on his arm, shouted out aloud:

"We have traveled the seas and wish to purchase slaves. Have you prepared any slaves to sell for us?"

"Be generous and you will have them!" sounded the agreed answer. "Come forth in peace!"

Now, the ships approached the shore, and when they reached the sand, the oarsmen rose and took hold of their spears and shields. Both captains jumped onto the sand, throwing their weapons upon the ground as a sign of peace, and walked up to the chieftain of the wilderness.

"We come in peace, O chieftain! Greetings to you and may your gods protect you from danger!"

"May your gods show kindness to you, O noble merchants!"

They bowed before him and greeted him with many gestures. The old man bowed his head in response.

"No doubt you must be tired. Let these skins containing fresh water be a gift to your people from mine."

"We thank you, O chieftain. And here is a necklace for your wife or daughter to hang around her beautiful neck if it should please you!"

One of the captains passed a glittering necklace to the warrior flanking his chieftain.

"Our craftsmen use a secret art to make objects as beautiful as these for our women and for the women of our friends."

The warrior gave the necklace to the chieftain, who glanced at it and passed it on.

"And now, be kind, both of you, and enter my abode, for you must nourish yourselves before inspecting the slaves you wish to purchase."

They moved on.

"We need young and healthy men," spoke one of the captains, "and also grown girls who can be of use. But if you have seized any old men or children, slay them, lest they should hinder you and partake of your food freely, for we have no interest in them, and moreover, neither will anyone else."

"My warriors do not wander the wilderness in order to waste their strength for nothing to bring across from very far away slaves that we cannot sell. Be patient. When your eyes rest upon our slaves, you will see for yourselves that in all your islands, there are none as suitable as these."

Now they drew near the village where most of its population was waiting. Warriors, women, children—all of them had gathered to look upon the strangers from the sea. As usual, the arrival of the merchants was a day of great celebration, for the women were offered gifts and the men new weapons, and everything the world could find was exchanged for slaves, which this miserable village, trapped between the sea of sand and the sea of waters, so readily provided.

When they had nourished themselves, the chieftain rose and led the two strangers to the edge of the village, where the slaves were held.

The guards signaled, and the captives all stood up, eyeing their future masters with great unease.

Both captains walked along the line of prisoners, carefully inspecting their naked bodies, for the slaves had been stripped naked for the inspection.

They stopped in front of one of them. A young slave with white hair and pale skin stood naked before them.

"Never could your land have fathered this creature!" spoke one of the captains looking at the chieftain. And then, waiting no longer, he spoke unto him in his native tongue:

"Who are you, and how have you found your way here?"

"I am the son of a fisherman, master. I was driven to this land by ill fortune and cast into bondage."

"Where is your home?"

"I am a subject of the king of Troy."

"Troy. I have heard of it. It is a city in the north."

"Yes, master."

"I am short one man, for fever gripped one of my oarsmen, and he perished on the seas. Can you row?"

"My father is a fisherman."

"You are not fully grown yet." he squeezed his upper arm to test his muscles. "But I shall take you. You are strong enough."

"Thank you, master!"

Whitehair bowed before him. His heart pounded, for he was filled with joy. But the chieftain raised his arm and shook his head.

"You can purchase them all, but not this one."

"As you wish, chieftain. An oarsman of mine has died, and this one here would be a good replacement, for he speaks our tongue. But let him remain where he stands if such is your will."

They moved on but stopped again, for the captain had opened the mouth of a girl standing behind Whitehair and started inspecting her teeth.

On the next day, a bargain was struck, and the slaves walked onto the ship, where they were crowded on the bare boards. Many days would they spend there before the journey would reach its end.

Two sails were hoisted. The oars dipped into the water, and both black ships moved along the shore and gradually drew further and further away.

The old chieftain ordered Whitehair to be taken into a windowless mud hut, for now he was the only one left in the enclosure. A warrior holding a spear in his hand sat behind a leather curtain covering the entrance. He probably did not know the tongue of the People of the Sea, for he uttered not a word to his prisoner. Whitehair wandered round the small room for a long time and at last threw himself upon the skins on the ground and fell asleep.

Now, during this time, the two black ships described a wide circle on the open waters and vanished behind the murky horizon. It was dusk already, a time when the nomads of the sea usually approached land to spend the night. But these ships remained motionless until six slender shapes emerged over the horizon to the west. And now their oars dipped into the water again, and both ships floated over the surface towards the new arrivals.

The ships approached each other and crowded together in such a way that a man could easily jump from one onto the next. And now eight leaders in all gathered on one of the ships.

"Tell us of what you saw, my son!" said a grey-haired seafarer, weaving a cuirass of dark metal which reflected no light at all, as if he wished his figure to remain concealed in darkness.

"It is a large settlement, father, just as you foresaw, and a great many men, women, and children dwell in it, any one of which could easily survive a journey by sea. They had several beautiful objects of gold and offered to trade them, but I refused, explaining that our commodities were of too little value to satisfy them. If two hundred of us fall upon them by surprise, not only shall we seize many slaves, but also the gold they have, and we will escape onto our ships before the rest of their warriors who wander the wilderness have time to return. And moreover, the gifts we offered for their slaves will be ours once more."

"How shall we assail them?"

"From the sea. The night will hide us as we approach the shore in one of our ships. A few of our more stealthy men will creep onto the land and slay the guards noiselessly, who keep watch over the village from a certain hill at the shore. Then we shall approach as close as possible before pouncing upon them. And if they are caught unawares, our gains will be great."

"It is a truly wise plan, my son!"

The ships scattered, weaving through the water which had taken on the appearance of dark wine, now that the sun was resting in its depths.

Whitehair woke up. He sat up straight and wiped his eyes. Night must have fallen, for he saw no light coming from the entrance beneath the curtain.

Sitting upon the floor, he reached for the mug of water and a barley cake which the guard had brought to him before nightfall. He closed his eyes. Why had the old chieftain refused to sell him to the people of the ships? Could he have learned somehow that the temple of Sebek was prepared to give much greater riches in exchange for him than the slave merchants could ever offer?

He covered his eyes with his hands. Suddenly he felt drained of all energy, left without the slightest hope of doing anything at all, and knowing that the time for hope, striving, and escape had gone forever.

"Mother... Mother..." he whispered, sobbing silently and biting his lips lest the guard should hear him, step inside, and witness such a contemptible sight.

At last, a calmness descended upon him. And now his thoughts, though they were full of despair, were no longer a storm tormenting his mind. If the gods wished it, he would perish. They had jeered him by guiding him as far as the coast which he had so much wished to see once more. And they had sent the two ships with people speaking his tongue and two captains with intentions of taking him on board to show him how close his escape was. But all this was for nothing.

Again he fell asleep.

But a while later, he was awoken by a shrill scream in the distance and sat up. Then someone else screamed, and suddenly a wild uproar surrounded the mud hut. Shrieking voices and groans became more and more frequent, and he heard many people running past his hut.

The young Trojan stepped towards the entrance and pulled the curtain back. The guard stood before him, and his spear was raised as he prepared to smite an approaching warrior wearing a helmet and panache which blew about in the wind.

Without thinking about his actions, Whitehair struck the guard upon the back of the head with all his might. For a while, the man's arm remained raised, brandishing the spear.

Only now did the one who was approaching realize what danger had threatened him in the gloom and struck the guard across the chest with a short, wide-bladed sword, causing him to stagger and fall with a thud.

Whitehair tore the spear out of the hands of the dying guard. The roof of the adjoining abode burst into flames, lighting his way, so that he could follow the assailants clad in cuirasses, but further on, he plunged into the darkness.

Where was the sea? In which direction? He ran out from amongst the mud huts.

An arrow swished past his ear and glided into the darkness. He fell onto the ground, looking about and gripping his spear all the while.

Against the background of leaping flames, he could see screaming women and children dragged into the darkness by men wearing helmets. And so now he knew where the attack had come from.

He stole along, following the assailants who were dragging away their captives but tried to keep out of the light of the burning houses.

Suddenly someone jumped out of the night: a dark-skinned, half-naked warrior. A great fear burnt in his eyes. He ran straight towards Whitehair, and when he noticed him, he brandished the dagger in his hand. The attack was so sudden and unexpected that the young Trojan only just managed to step back and thrust his spear, piercing his attacker's chest. He tried to tear it out, but it had entered the man's body very deep, and when he pulled at it again, the spear snapped. The one he had slain fell to the ground.

Whitehair bent down, took hold of the dagger, and leaped aside, for he saw the shadow of another warrior approaching with a sword in his hand.

He clung to the trunk of a tall palm tree and tried to understand the situation. The abode of the chieftain stood just opposite him. He was sure of this, for two warriors wearing helmets with panaches, which he recognized as the People of the Sea, were dragging the old chieftain from out of his dwelling. One of them lifted his sword and slew the old man on the spot, and the other one entered the abode once more, returning with a white linen packet.

"Retreat, retreat!" a loud voice pierced the night, and the call was repeated by other mouths.

Those wearing helmets turned around and started running. He moved after them.

A new vigor had entered the veins of the villagers, for those warriors who had fled into the wilderness at the first attack through fear were now returning. The retreating seafarers were now followed by the hiss of arrows.

Fearing that the warriors from the sea, with whom he wished to escape, would slay him on sight, he carefully advanced in the darkness, but when he left the trees and walked out onto the beach, he knew he could not avoid being seen any longer.

"Wait! Wait! Take me with you!" he shouted and threw himself forward, staggering through the sand after them. Two arrows zipped past him, then another two. But the fifth one he did not hear.

A sharp pain bit his leg and he fell down, but soon he scrambled back up again, though he felt that an arrow had lodged in his thigh. He reached behind him and pulled it out, sensing that a piece of flesh had come away with it, and stumbled along towards the water.

The ships were close to shore upon the water, and men were scrambling on board. Using all their might, they climbed up ropes hanging down the black hulls and, jumping in, took hold of the oars.

Whitehair dove into the water. Beating madly with his arms and feeling his right leg growing weaker and hindering him more and more, he swam for a dark shape ahead of him.

"Wait!" he screamed, but he sensed it was all in vain, and even if they did mistake him for one of their own in the dark, they would not turn back to collect him, for the shore was already swarming with a multitude of figures, and the air above the ship was whistling with arrows.

With a desperate effort, he threw himself forward, sweeping the water aside with powerful strokes. And suddenly the ship was much closer. He stretched out an arm grasping for an oar.

Two dark silhouettes loomed out from above, and two pairs of powerful hands gripped him.

He stretched up, placed his other hand upon the side of the ship, and tumbled down onto the feet of the men crowding the deck.

A huge sail suddenly unfurled overhead and swelled out with the offshore wind which always blew at night.

END OF VOLUME ONE

Other great books from Mondrala Press

Witold Makowiecki
Out of the Lion's Maw

A European action-adventure bestseller set in the ancient Mediterranean. An elderly Zoroastrian priest and his teen apprentice try to prevent the outbreak of a civil war in Egypt. Their opponent is the entire state apparatus of Eternal Egypt. Their resources: the old man's wit and the young man's courage.

"I can't believe it has taken 75 years for this story to be made available in English!"

Witold Makowiecki
Wind from the Hospitable Sea

In extraordinary times, twelve-year-old boys must act like men. Greece 562 B.C. For insolvent debtors, the price of bankruptcy is slavery. When his mother and siblings are seized for unpaid debts, little Diossos must run to fetch help. He must cross mountains, forests, and stormy seas, brave wild animals, slave catchers, pirates, and—police. He has a month to achieve his quest, only days to grow up.

"Such an epic adventure!"

Other Volumes of the Roman Trilogy

Jacek Bocheński
Divine Julius

Would you like to become a god? It is perfectly doable.
So starts this fascinating glimpse into the mind of Julius Caesar and his opponents, written in a terse style imitating Caesar's own. A great critical and commercial success when it first appeared, the book was soon banned by the communist regime because it portrayed a little too clearly how a tyranny manufactures consent.
"A fillet mignon of prose, it has to be savored!"

Jacek Bocheński
Tiberius Caesar

Who was the man who ruled Rome between A.D. 14 and 37? A cruel freak or a misunderstood loner? A journey to Capri, Rhodes, and Rome, taking in both the then and the now. Anecdotes, dialogue scenes, Tiberius' internal monologues, historians' voices, and the author's timeless reflections.

Other great books from Monarala Press

Aleksander Krawczuk
Seven Against Thebes

Before the Trojan War there was the Theban War. One of Europe's best-selling authors of popular books on Graeco-Roman antiquity discusses in a delightfully conversational style the Greek myth of Seven Against Thebes, its roots in the Bronze Age, and its impact on subsequent generations of Greeks and Romans.
"A classicist's escapist dream!"

Maria Rodziewiczówna
A Summer of the Forest Folk

A classic feel-good story of friendship, coming of age and the healing power of nature. Three women spend each summer in a remote cottage in the last virgin forest of Europe. This summer, they are joined by their big city nephew.
"Irresistibly charming!"

Made in United States
North Haven, CT
14 February 2023

32600215R00104